POKéMON ™

BLACK AND WHITE

VOL.6

Story by **HIDENORI KUSAKA**
Art by **SATOSHI YAMAMOTO**

Pokémon Black and White
Volume 6
VIZ Kids Edition

Story by HIDENORI KUSAKA
Art by SATOSHI YAMAMOTO

© 2012 Pokémon.
© 1995-2011 Nintendo/Creatures Inc./GAME FREAK inc.
TM and ® and character names are trademarks of Nintendo.
© 1997 Hidenori KUSAKA and Satoshi YAMAMOTO/Shogakukan
All rights reserved.
Original Japanese edition "POCKET MONSTER SPECIAL"
published by SHOGAKUKAN Inc.

English Adaptation / Annette Roman
Translation / Tetsuichiro Miyaki
Touch-up & Lettering / Susan Daigle-Leach
Design / Fawn Lau
Cover Colorist / Genki Hagata
Editor / Annette Roman

Printed in the U.S.A.

Published by VIZ Media, LLC
P.O. Box 77010
San Francisco, CA 94107

10 9 8 7 6 5 4 3 2 1
First printing, March 2012

PARENTAL ADVISORY
POKÉMON ADVENTURES
is rated A and is suitable
for readers of all ages.
ratings.viz.com

www.vizkids.com   www.viz.com

POKÉMON™

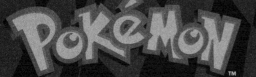

BLACK AND WHITE

VOL. 6

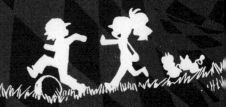

THE STORY THUS FAR!

Pokémon Trainer Black is exploring the mysterious Unova Region with his brand-new Pokédex. Pokémon Trainer White runs a thriving talent agency for performing Pokémon. Now she has hired Black as her assistant. Meanwhile, Team Plasma is plotting to separate Pokémon from their beloved humans...!

BLACK'S dream is to win the Pokémon League!

WHITE'S dream is to make her Tepig Gigi a star!

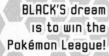

Black's Tepig, TEP, and White's Tepig, GIGI, get along like peanut butter and jelly!

Black's Munna, MUSHA, helps him think clearly by temporarily "eating" his dream.

Adventure 18
Big-City Battles

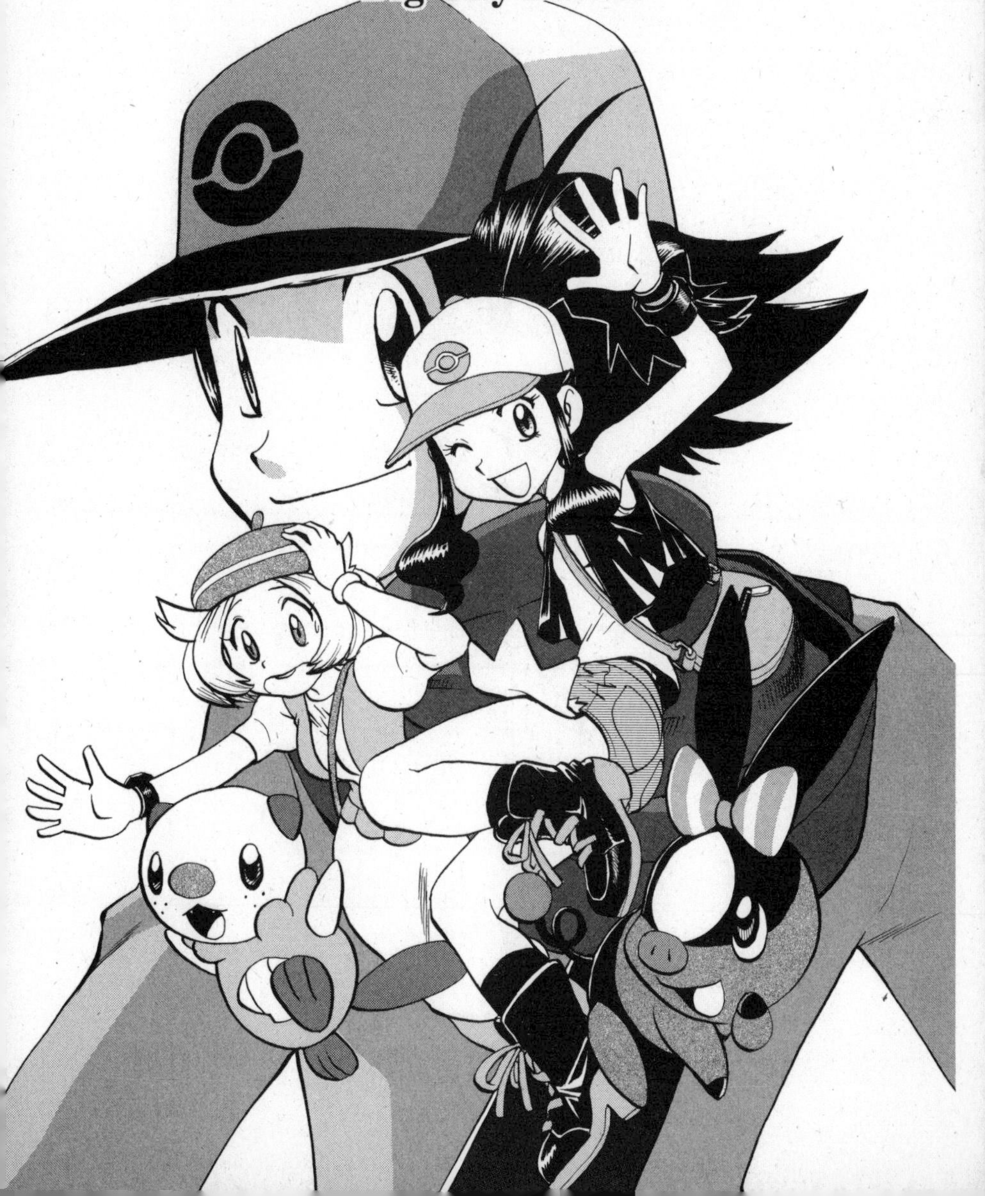

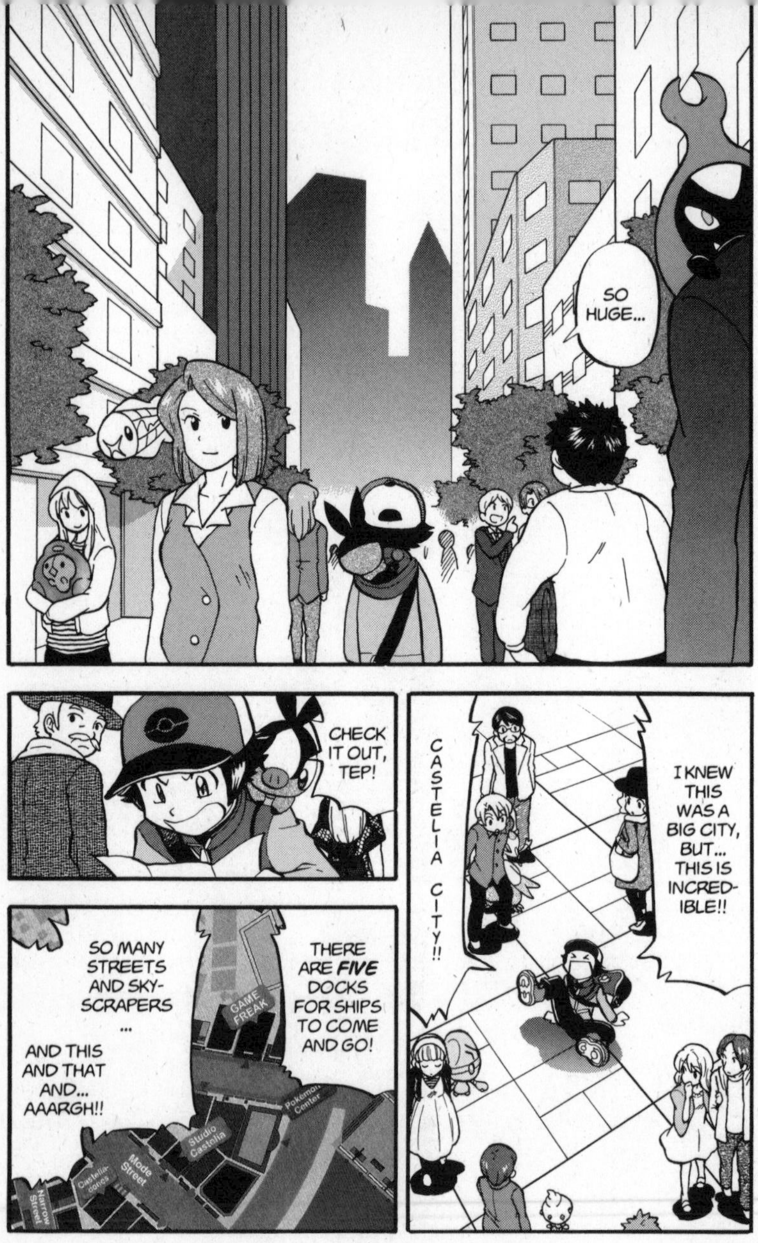
SO HUGE...
CHECK IT OUT, TEP!
CASTELIA CITY!!
I KNEW THIS WAS A BIG CITY, BUT... THIS IS INCREDIBLE!!
SO MANY STREETS AND SKY-SCRAPERS...
THERE ARE ***FIVE*** DOCKS FOR SHIPS TO COME AND GO!
AND THIS AND THAT AND... AAARGH!!
GAME FREAK
Pokémon Center
Studio Castelia
Mode Street
Castelia-cones
Narrow Street

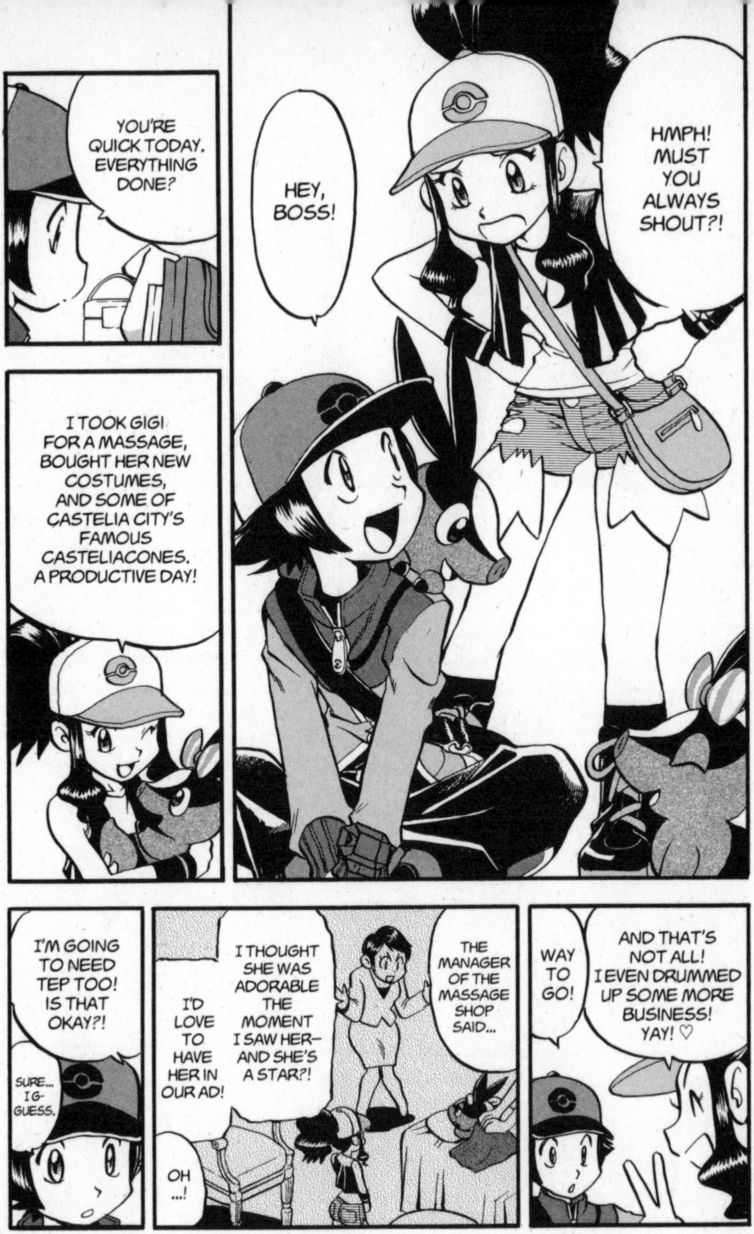
YOU'RE QUICK TODAY. EVERYTHING DONE?
HEY, BOSS!
HMPH! MUST YOU ALWAYS SHOUT?!
I TOOK GIGI FOR A MASSAGE, BOUGHT HER NEW COSTUMES, AND SOME OF CASTELIA CITY'S FAMOUS CASTELIACONES. A PRODUCTIVE DAY!
I'M GOING TO NEED TEP TOO! IS THAT OKAY?!
SURE... I G-GUESS.
I THOUGHT SHE WAS ADORABLE THE MOMENT I SAW HER—AND SHE'S A STAR?!
I'D LOVE TO HAVE HER IN OUR AD!
OH ...!
THE MANAGER OF THE MASSAGE SHOP SAID...
WAY TO GO!
AND THAT'S NOT ALL! I EVEN DRUMMED UP SOME MORE BUSINESS! YAY! ♡

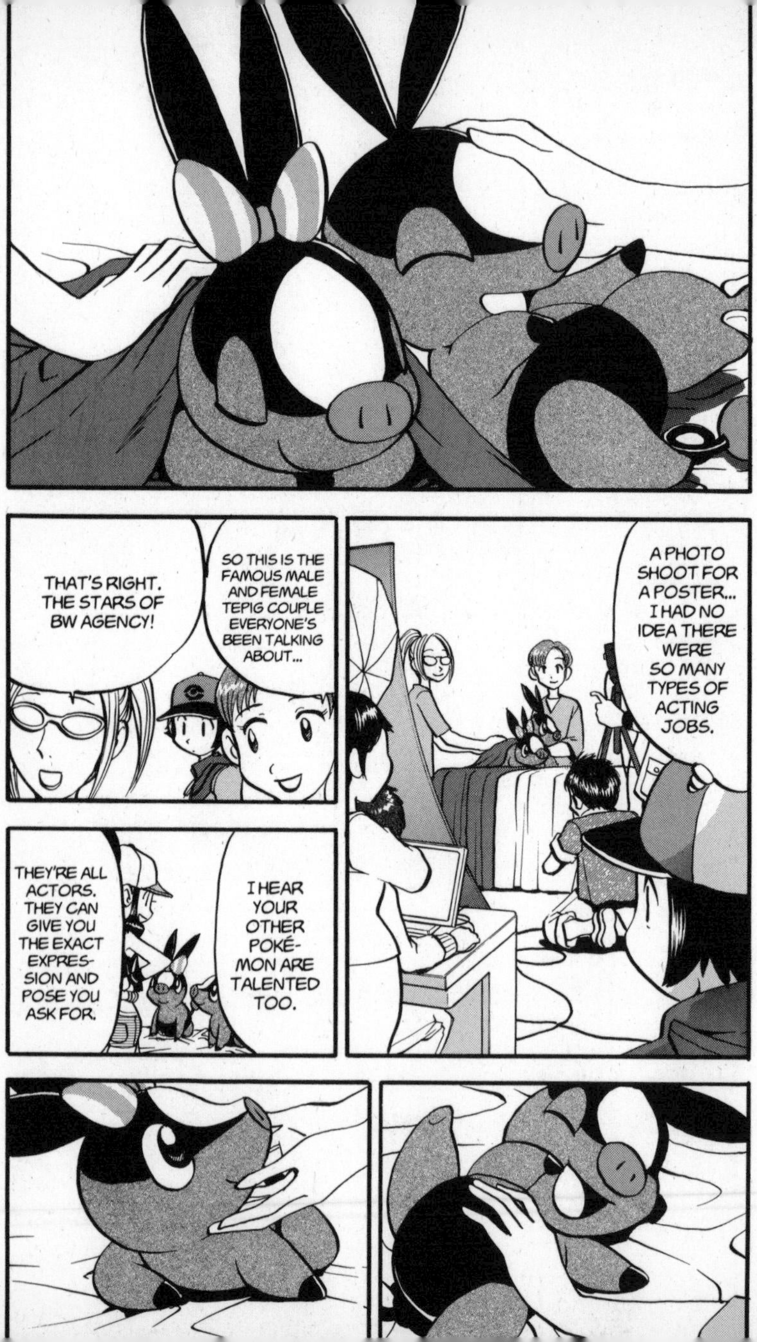
A PHOTO SHOOT FOR A POSTER... I HAD NO IDEA THERE WERE SO MANY TYPES OF ACTING JOBS.
SO THIS IS THE FAMOUS MALE AND FEMALE TEPIG COUPLE EVERYONE'S BEEN TALKING ABOUT...
THAT'S RIGHT. THE STARS OF BW AGENCY!
I HEAR YOUR OTHER POKÉMON ARE TALENTED TOO.
THEY'RE ALL ACTORS. THEY CAN GIVE YOU THE EXACT EXPRESSION AND POSE YOU ASK FOR.

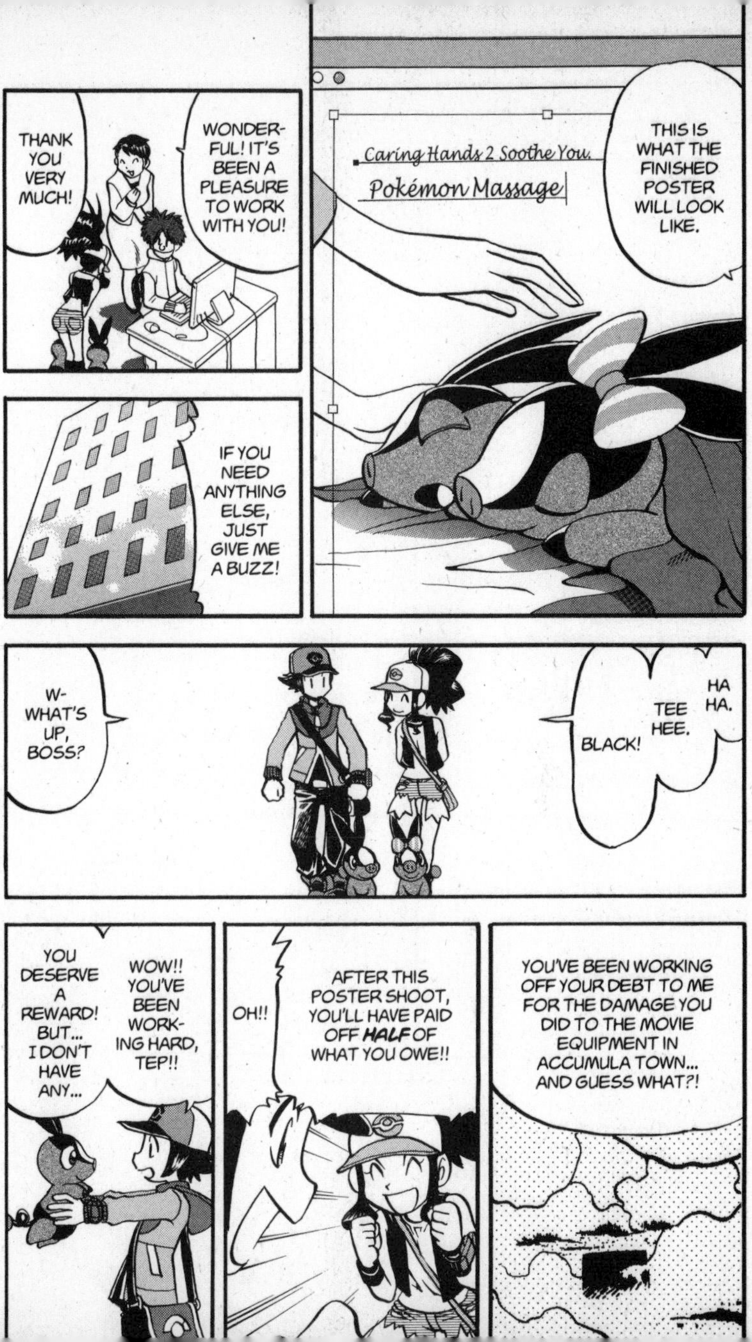
THIS IS WHAT THE FINISHED POSTER WILL LOOK LIKE.
Caring Hands 2 Soothe You.
Pokémon Massage
WONDERFUL! IT'S BEEN A PLEASURE TO WORK WITH YOU!
THANK YOU VERY MUCH!
IF YOU NEED ANYTHING ELSE, JUST GIVE ME A BUZZ!
HA HA.
TEE HEE.
BLACK!
W-WHAT'S UP, BOSS?
YOU'VE BEEN WORKING OFF YOUR DEBT TO ME FOR THE DAMAGE YOU DID TO THE MOVIE EQUIPMENT IN ACCUMULA TOWN... AND GUESS WHAT?!
AFTER THIS POSTER SHOOT, YOU'LL HAVE PAID OFF HALF OF WHAT YOU OWE!!
OH!!
WOW!! YOU'VE BEEN WORKING HARD, TEP!!
YOU DESERVE A REWARD! BUT... I DON'T HAVE ANY...

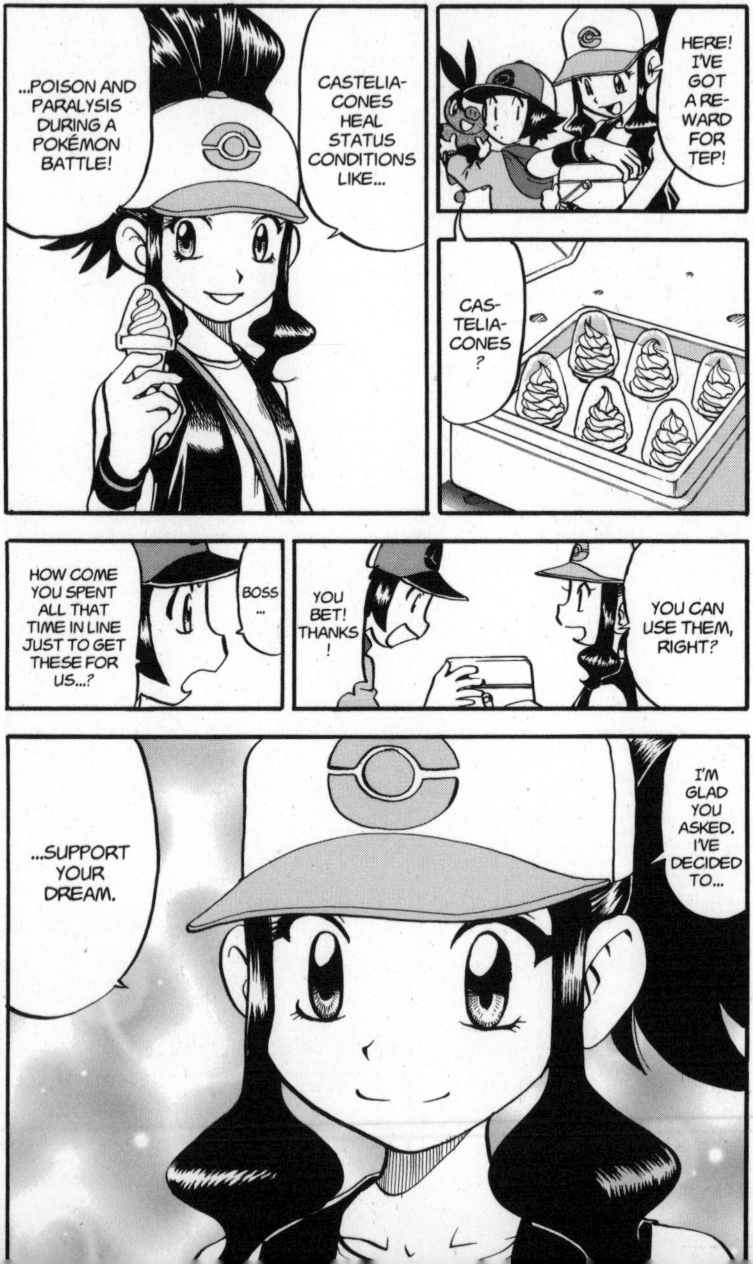
HERE! I'VE GOT A REWARD FOR TEP!
CASTELIA-CONES?
CASTELIA-CONES HEAL STATUS CONDITIONS LIKE...
...POISON AND PARALYSIS DURING A POKÉMON BATTLE!
YOU CAN USE THEM, RIGHT?
YOU BET! THANKS!
BOSS...
HOW COME YOU SPENT ALL THAT TIME IN LINE JUST TO GET THESE FOR US...?
I'M GLAD YOU ASKED. I'VE DECIDED TO...
...SUPPORT YOUR DREAM.

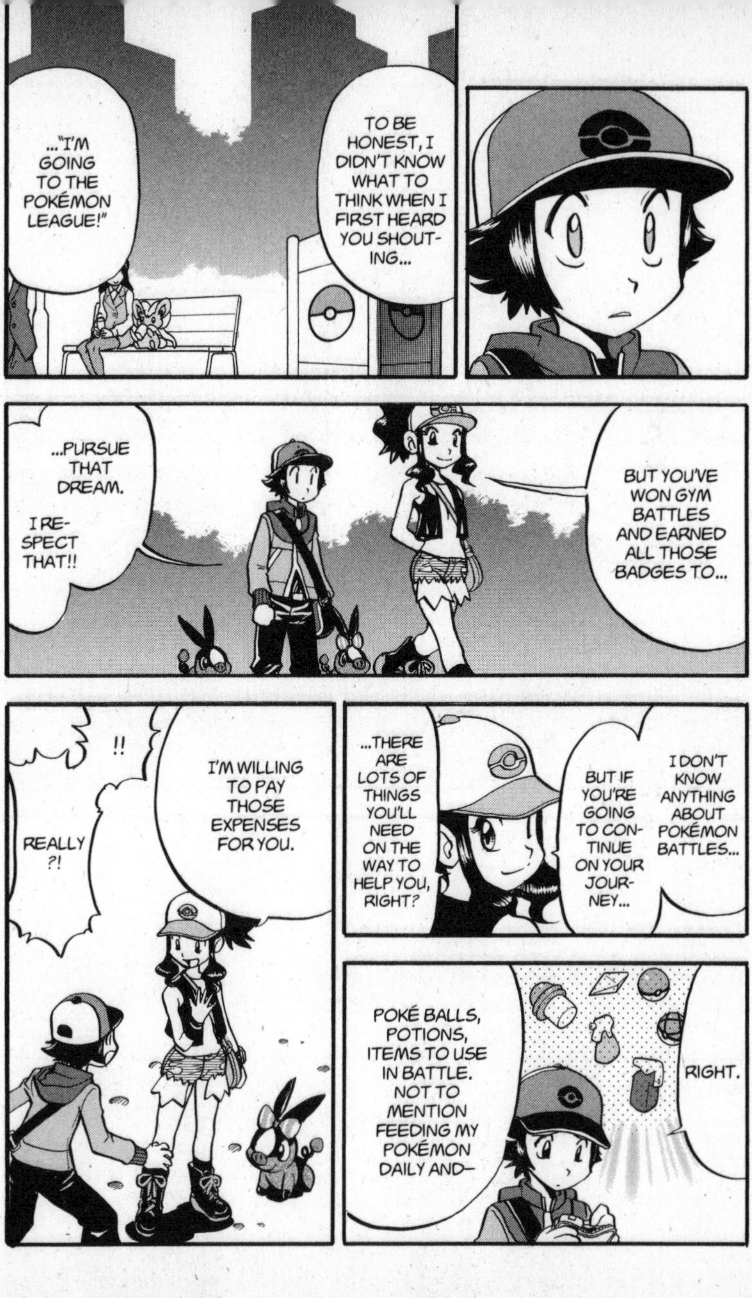
TO BE HONEST, I DIDN'T KNOW WHAT TO THINK WHEN I FIRST HEARD YOU SHOUTING...
..."I'M GOING TO THE POKÉMON LEAGUE!"
BUT YOU'VE WON GYM BATTLES AND EARNED ALL THOSE BADGES TO...
...PURSUE THAT DREAM.
I RESPECT THAT!!
I DON'T KNOW ANYTHING ABOUT POKÉMON BATTLES...
BUT IF YOU'RE GOING TO CONTINUE ON YOUR JOURNEY...
...THERE ARE LOTS OF THINGS YOU'LL NEED ON THE WAY TO HELP YOU, RIGHT?
RIGHT.
POKÉ BALLS, POTIONS, ITEMS TO USE IN BATTLE. NOT TO MENTION FEEDING MY POKÉMON DAILY AND—
I'M WILLING TO PAY THOSE EXPENSES FOR YOU.
!!
REALLY ?!

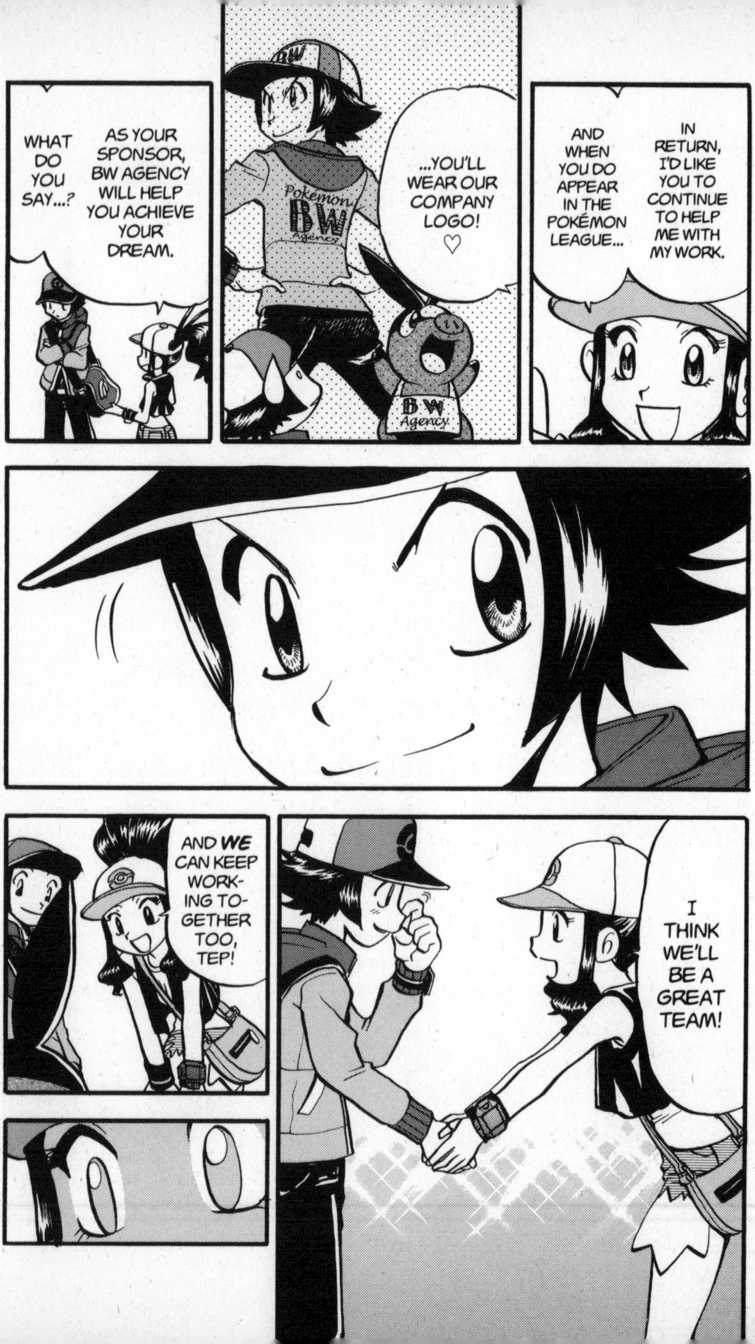
AS YOUR SPONSOR, BW AGENCY WILL HELP YOU ACHIEVE YOUR DREAM.
WHAT DO YOU SAY...?
...YOU'LL WEAR OUR COMPANY LOGO! ♡
Pokemon BW Agency
BW Agency
IN RETURN, I'D LIKE YOU TO CONTINUE TO HELP ME WITH MY WORK.
AND WHEN YOU DO APPEAR IN THE POKÉMON LEAGUE...
I THINK WE'LL BE A GREAT TEAM!
AND **WE** CAN KEEP WORKING TOGETHER TOO, TEP!

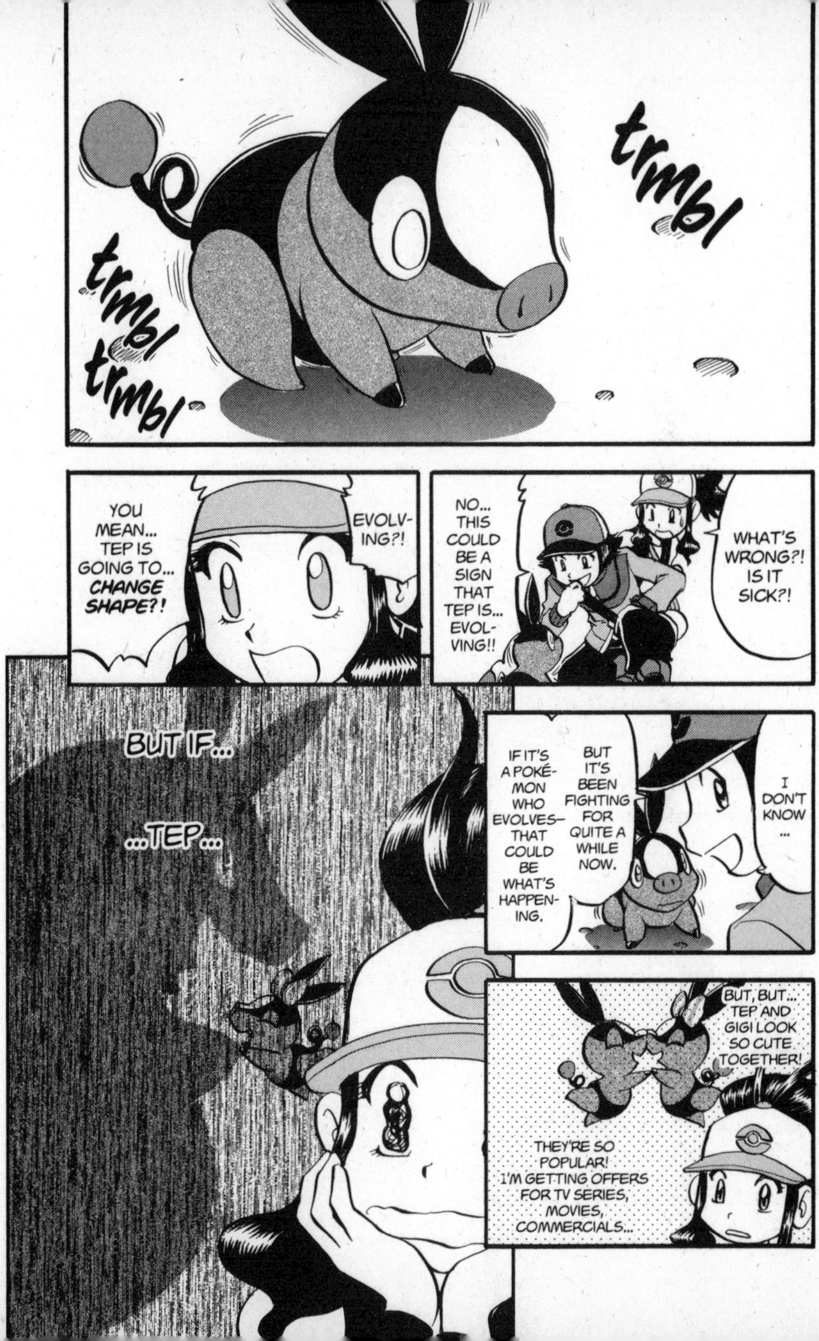
trmbl
trmbl trmbl
WHAT'S WRONG?! IS IT SICK?!
NO... THIS COULD BE A SIGN THAT TEP IS... EVOLVING!!
EVOLVING?!
YOU MEAN... TEP IS GOING TO... CHANGE SHAPE?!
I DON'T KNOW...
BUT IT'S BEEN FIGHTING FOR QUITE A WHILE NOW.
IF IT'S A POKÉMON WHO EVOLVES—THAT COULD BE WHAT'S HAPPENING.
BUT, BUT... TEP AND GIGI LOOK SO CUTE TOGETHER!
THEY'RE SO POPULAR! I'M GETTING OFFERS FOR TV SERIES, MOVIES, COMMERCIALS...
BUT IF...
...TEP...

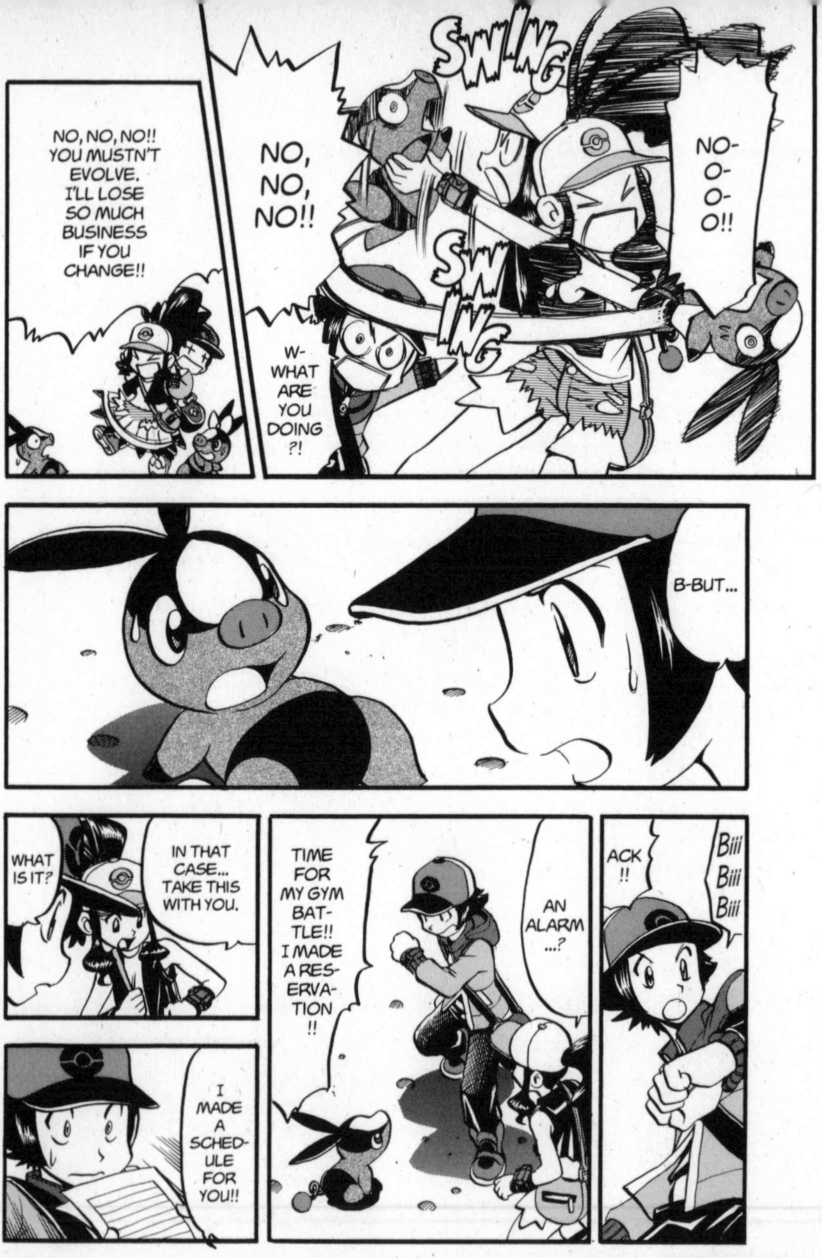
NO, NO, NO!! YOU MUSTN'T EVOLVE. I'LL LOSE SO MUCH BUSINESS IF YOU CHANGE!!
NO, NO, NO!!
SWING
NO-O-O-O!!
SWING SWING
W-WHAT ARE YOU DOING?!
B-BUT...
WHAT IS IT?
IN THAT CASE... TAKE THIS WITH YOU.
I MADE A SCHEDULE FOR YOU!!
TIME FOR MY GYM BATTLE!! I MADE A RESERVATION!!
AN ALARM...?
ACK!!
Biii Biii Biii

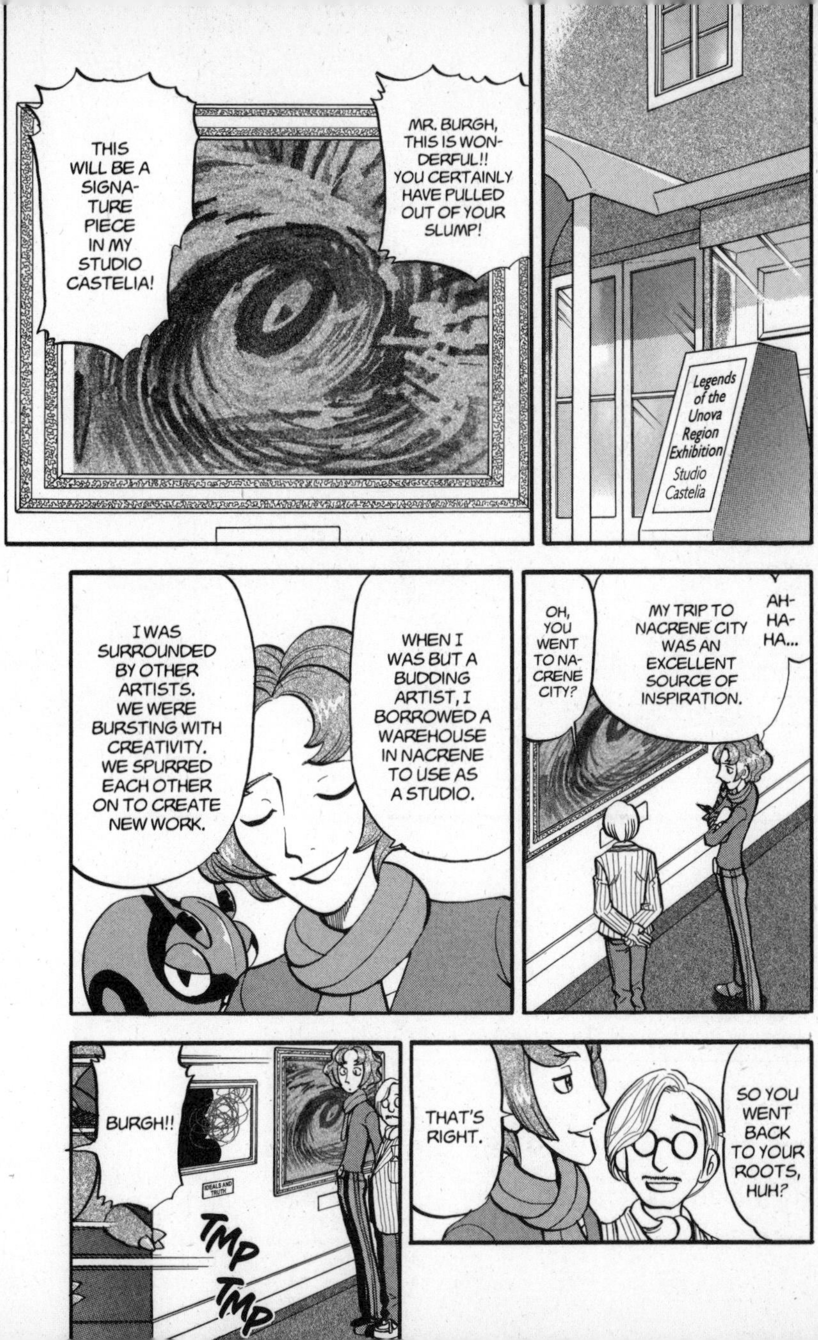
Legends of the Unova Region Exhibition
Studio Castelia
MR. BURGH, THIS IS WONDERFUL!! YOU CERTAINLY HAVE PULLED OUT OF YOUR SLUMP!
THIS WILL BE A SIGNATURE PIECE IN MY STUDIO CASTELIA!
AH-HA-HA...
MY TRIP TO NACRENE CITY WAS AN EXCELLENT SOURCE OF INSPIRATION.
OH, YOU WENT TO NACRENE CITY?
WHEN I WAS BUT A BUDDING ARTIST, I BORROWED A WAREHOUSE IN NACRENE TO USE AS A STUDIO.
I WAS SURROUNDED BY OTHER ARTISTS. WE WERE BURSTING WITH CREATIVITY. WE SPURRED EACH OTHER ON TO CREATE NEW WORK.
SO YOU WENT BACK TO YOUR ROOTS, HUH?
THAT'S RIGHT.
BURGH!!
IDEALS AND TRUTH
TMP TMP

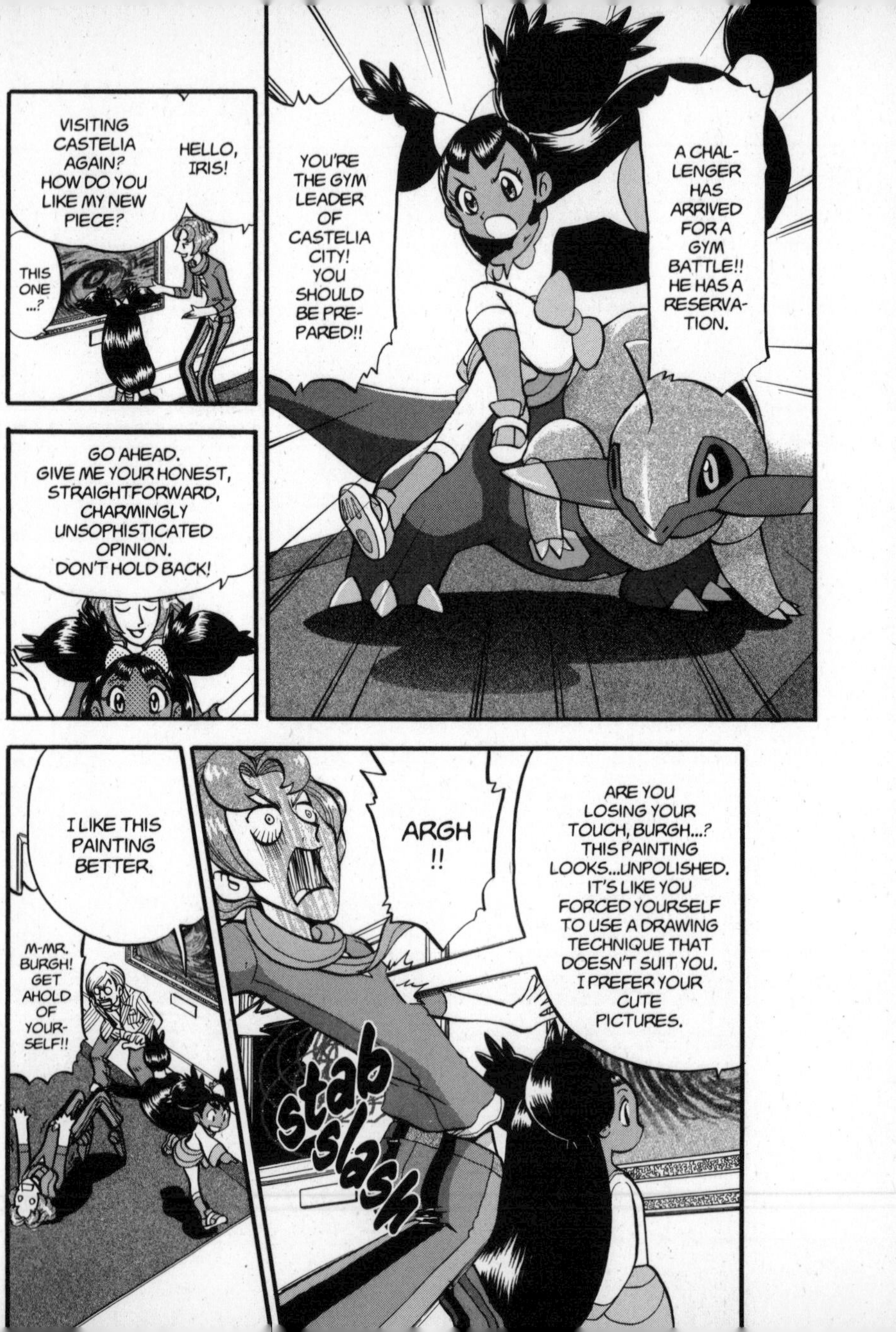
HELLO, IRIS!
VISITING CASTELIA AGAIN? HOW DO YOU LIKE MY NEW PIECE?
THIS ONE ...?
GO AHEAD. GIVE ME YOUR HONEST, STRAIGHTFORWARD, CHARMINGLY UNSOPHISTICATED OPINION. DON'T HOLD BACK!
YOU'RE THE GYM LEADER OF CASTELIA CITY! YOU SHOULD BE PRE-PARED!!
A CHAL-LENGER HAS ARRIVED FOR A GYM BATTLE!! HE HAS A RESERVA-TION.
ARE YOU LOSING YOUR TOUCH, BURGH...? THIS PAINTING LOOKS...UNPOLISHED. IT'S LIKE YOU FORCED YOURSELF TO USE A DRAWING TECHNIQUE THAT DOESN'T SUIT YOU. I PREFER YOUR CUTE PICTURES.
I LIKE THIS PAINTING BETTER.
ARGH !!
M-MR. BURGH! GET AHOLD OF YOUR-SELF!!
stab
slash

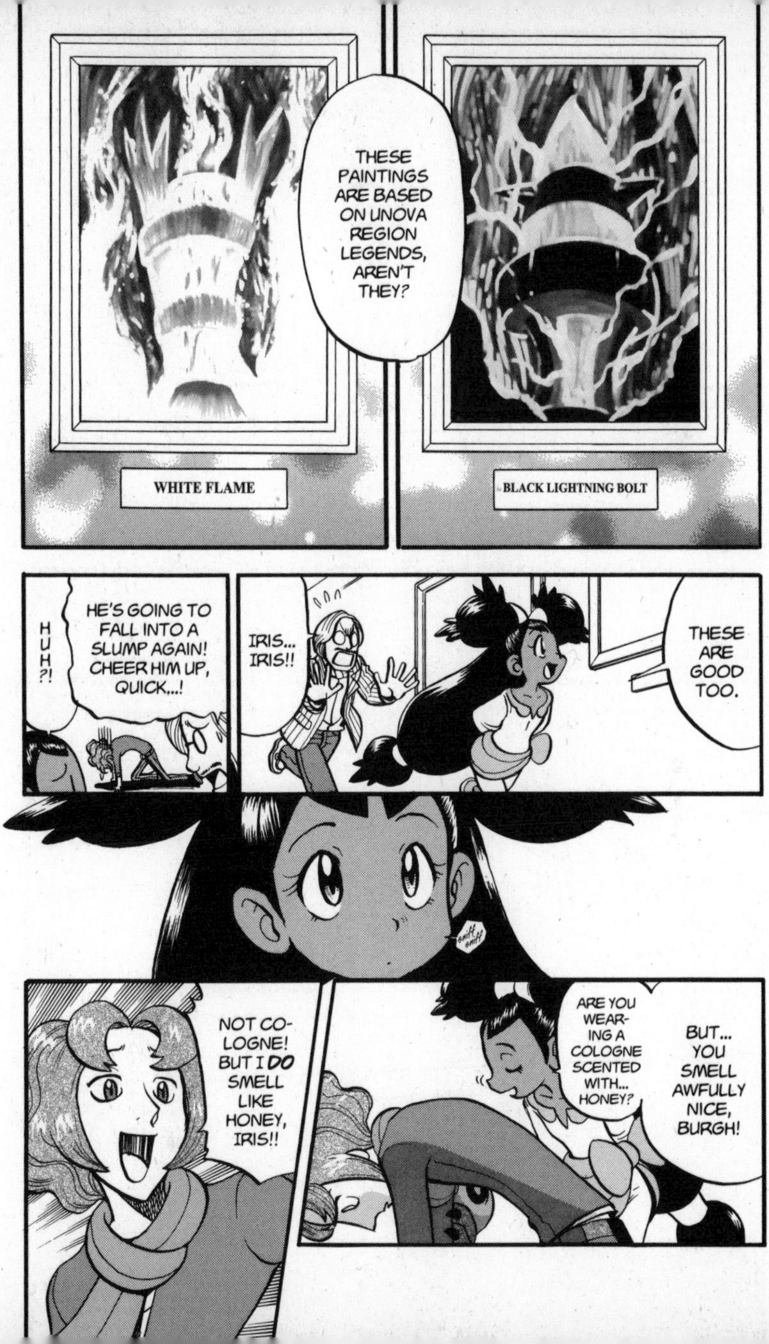
THESE PAINTINGS ARE BASED ON UNOVA REGION LEGENDS, AREN'T THEY?
WHITE FLAME
BLACK LIGHTNING BOLT
THESE ARE GOOD TOO.
IRIS... IRIS!!
HE'S GOING TO FALL INTO A SLUMP AGAIN! CHEER HIM UP, QUICK...!
HUH?!
sniff sniff
BUT... YOU SMELL AWFULLY NICE, BURGH!
ARE YOU WEAR-ING A COLOGNE SCENTED WITH... HONEY?
NOT CO-LOGNE! BUT I DO SMELL LIKE HONEY, IRIS!!

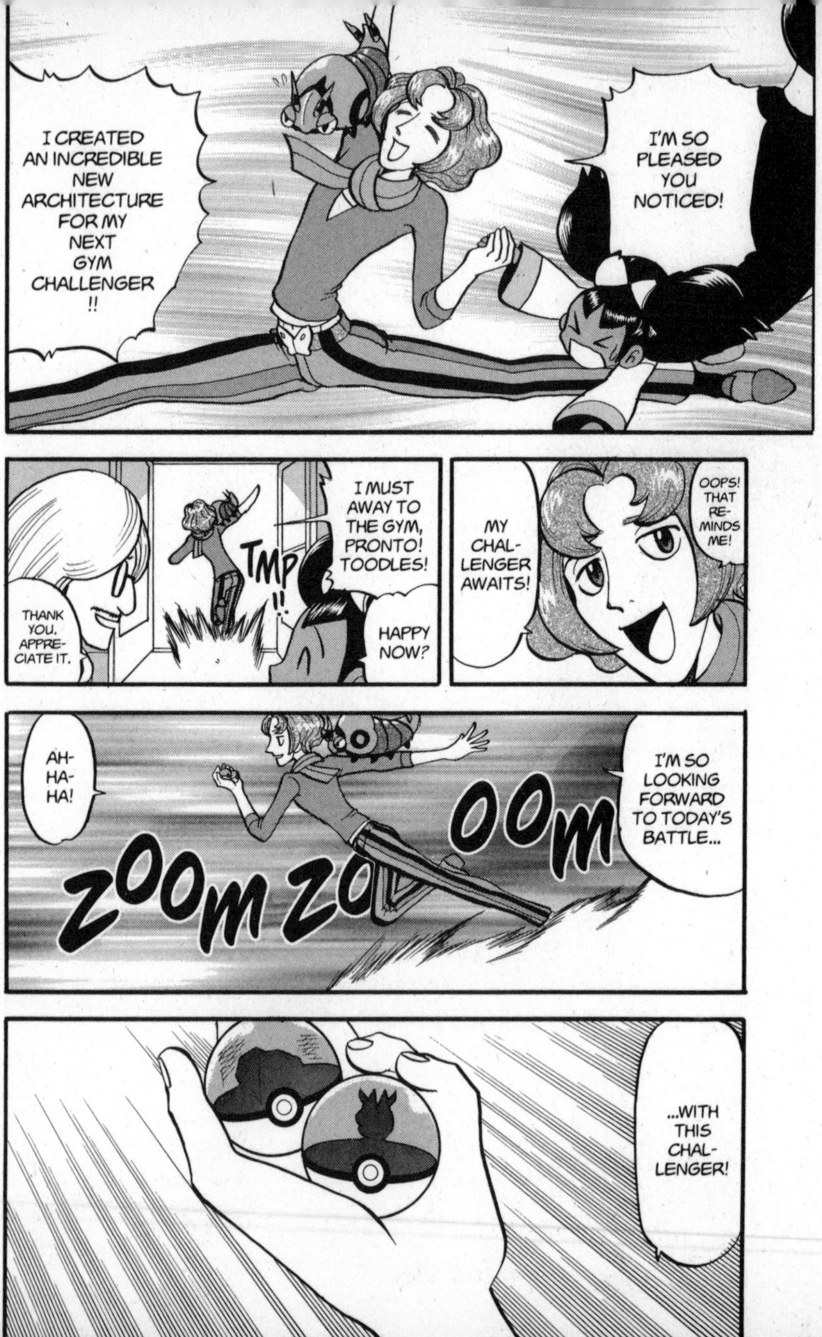
I'M SO PLEASED YOU NOTICED!
I CREATED AN INCREDIBLE NEW ARCHITECTURE FOR MY NEXT GYM CHALLENGER!!
OOPS! THAT RE-MINDS ME!
MY CHAL-LENGER AWAITS!
I MUST AWAY TO THE GYM, PRONTO! TOODLES!
TMP!!
HAPPY NOW?
THANK YOU. APPRE-CIATE IT.
I'M SO LOOKING FORWARD TO TODAY'S BATTLE...
AH-HA-HA!
ZOOM ZOOOM
...WITH THIS CHAL-LENGER!

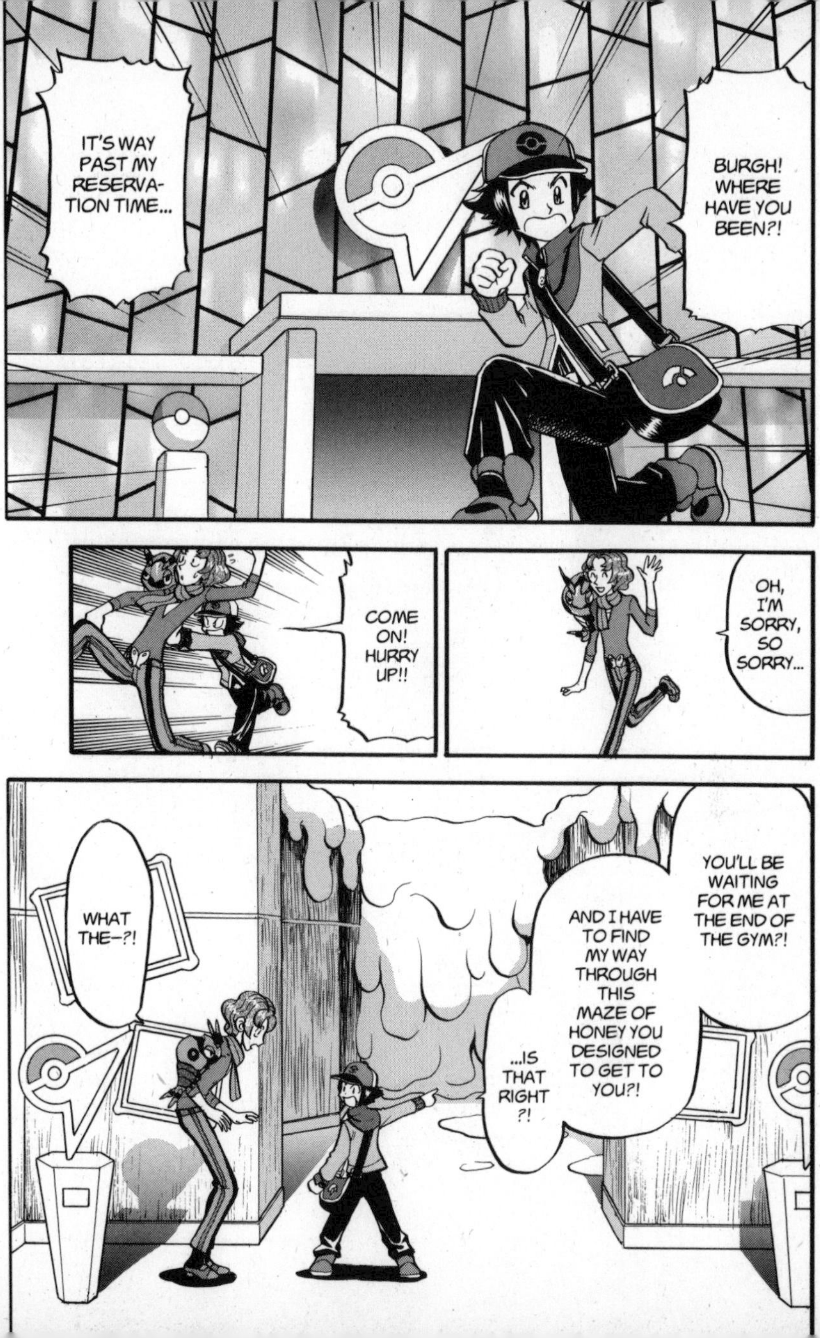
IT'S WAY PAST MY RESERVA-TION TIME...
BURGH! WHERE HAVE YOU BEEN?!
COME ON! HURRY UP!!
OH, I'M SORRY, SO SORRY...
WHAT THE-?!
YOU'LL BE WAITING FOR ME AT THE END OF THE GYM?!
AND I HAVE TO FIND MY WAY THROUGH THIS MAZE OF HONEY YOU DESIGNED TO GET TO YOU?!
...IS THAT RIGHT?!

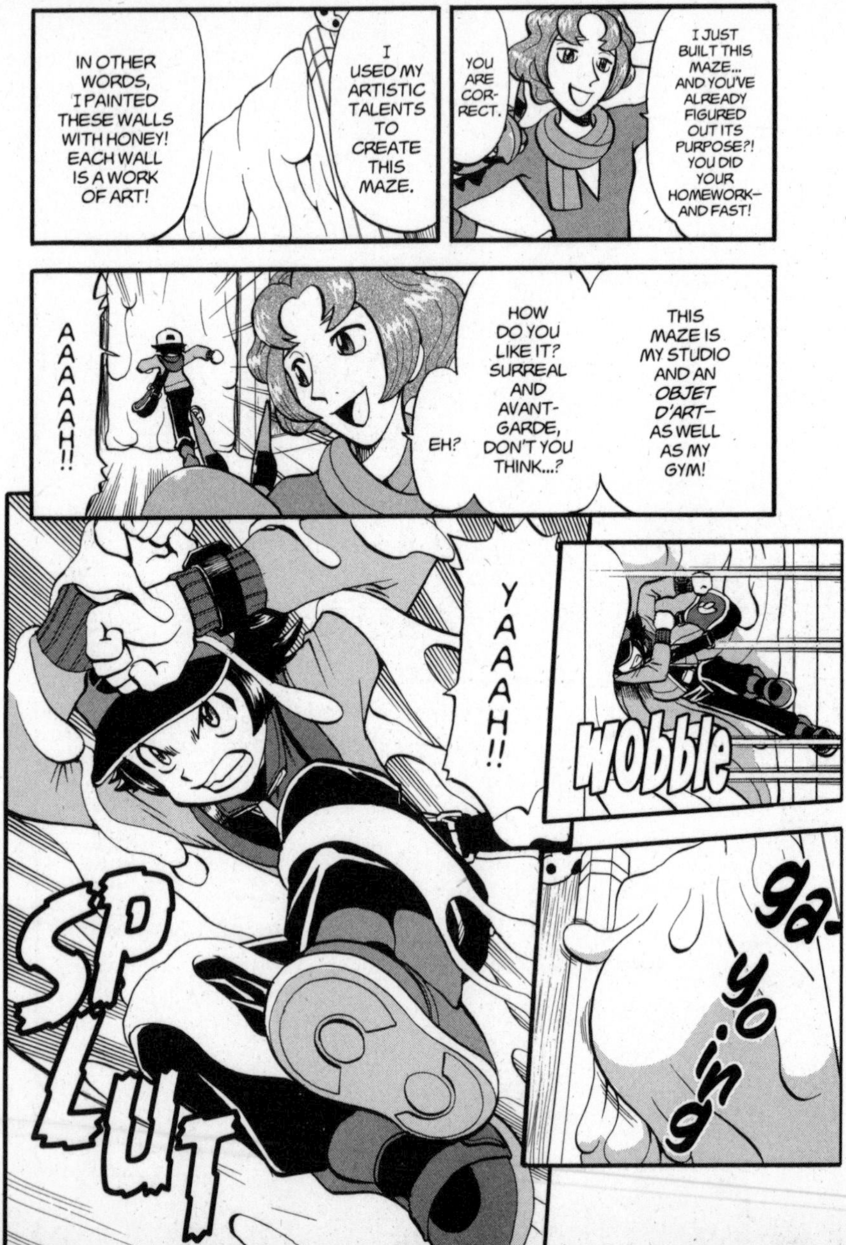

IN OTHER WORDS, I PAINTED THESE WALLS WITH HONEY! EACH WALL IS A WORK OF ART!
I USED MY ARTISTIC TALENTS TO CREATE THIS MAZE.
YOU ARE COR-RECT.
I JUST BUILT THIS MAZE... AND YOU'VE ALREADY FIGURED OUT ITS PURPOSE?! YOU DID YOUR HOMEWORK–AND FAST!
AAAAAAH!!
EH?
HOW DO YOU LIKE IT? SURREAL AND AVANT-GARDE, DON'T YOU THINK...?
THIS MAZE IS MY STUDIO AND AN OBJET D'ART–AS WELL AS MY GYM!
YAAAAH!!
wobble
SPLUT
ga-yo ing

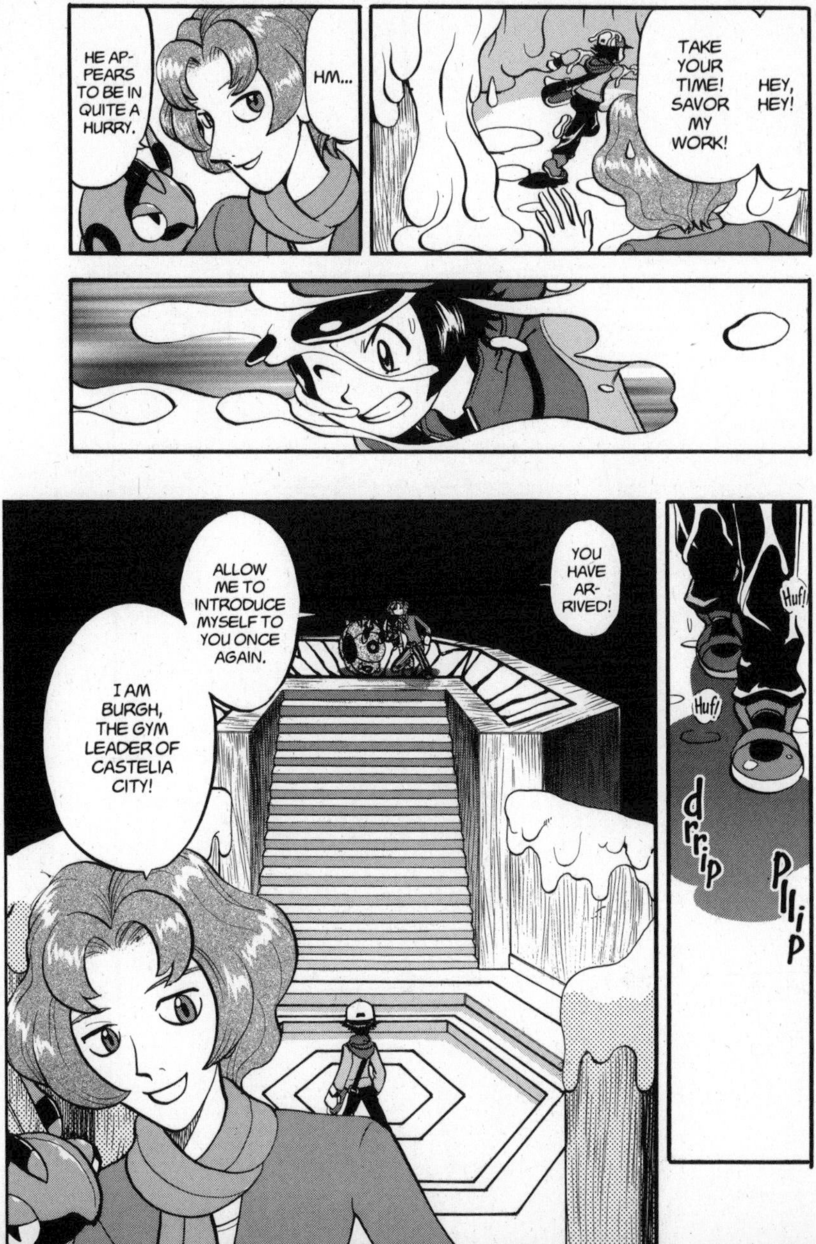
HE AP-PEARS TO BE IN QUITE A HURRY.
HM...
TAKE YOUR TIME! SAVOR MY WORK!
HEY, HEY!
Huf!
Huf!
drrip
Pllip
YOU HAVE AR-RIVED!
ALLOW ME TO INTRODUCE MYSELF TO YOU ONCE AGAIN.
I AM BURGH, THE GYM LEADER OF CASTELIA CITY!

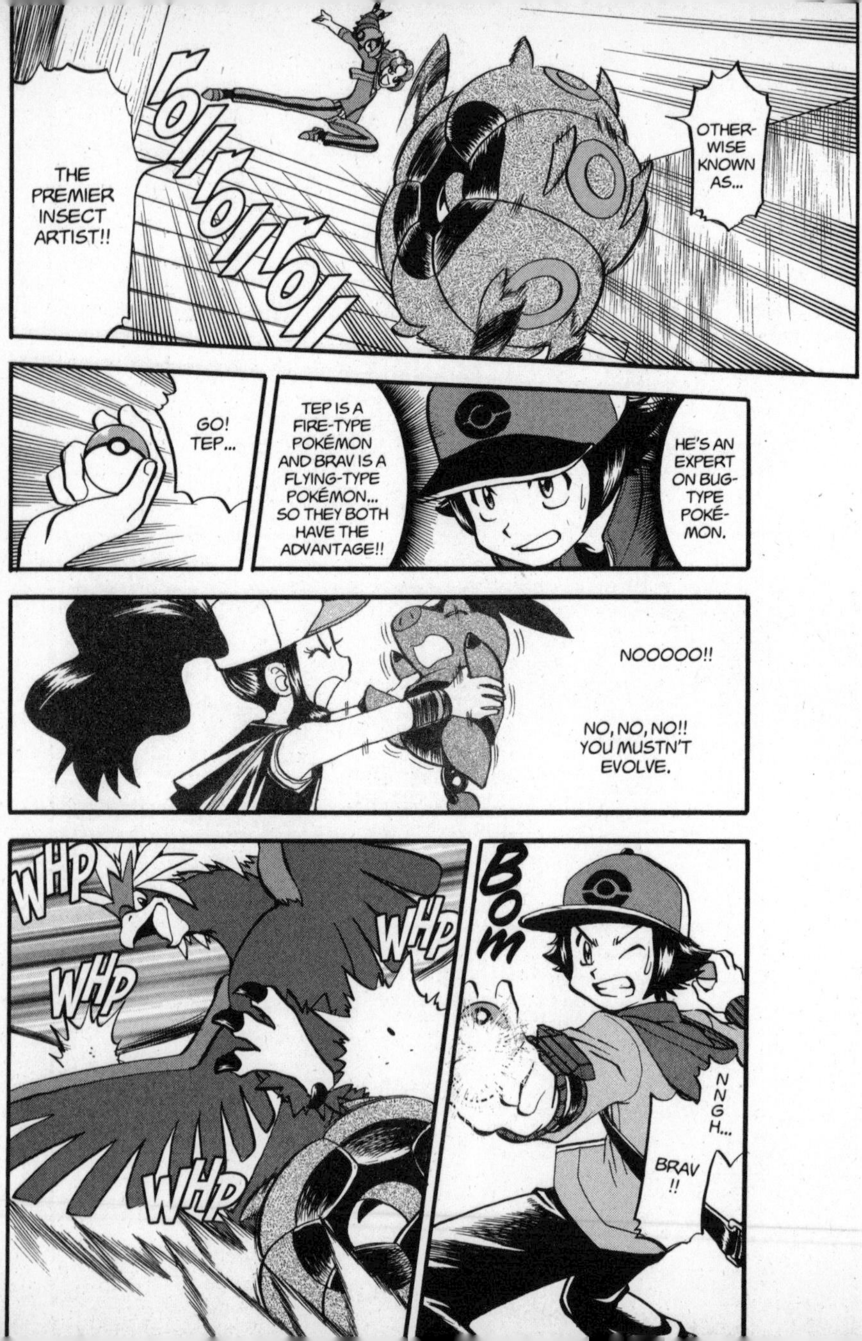
rollroll
OTHER-WISE KNOWN AS...
THE PREMIER INSECT ARTIST!!
HE'S AN EXPERT ON BUG-TYPE POKÉ-MON.
TEP IS A FIRE-TYPE POKÉMON AND BRAV IS A FLYING-TYPE POKÉMON... SO THEY BOTH HAVE THE ADVANTAGE!!
GO! TEP...
NOOOOO!!
NO, NO, NO!! YOU MUSTN'T EVOLVE.
Boom
NNGH...
BRAV!!
WHP
WHP
WHP
WHP

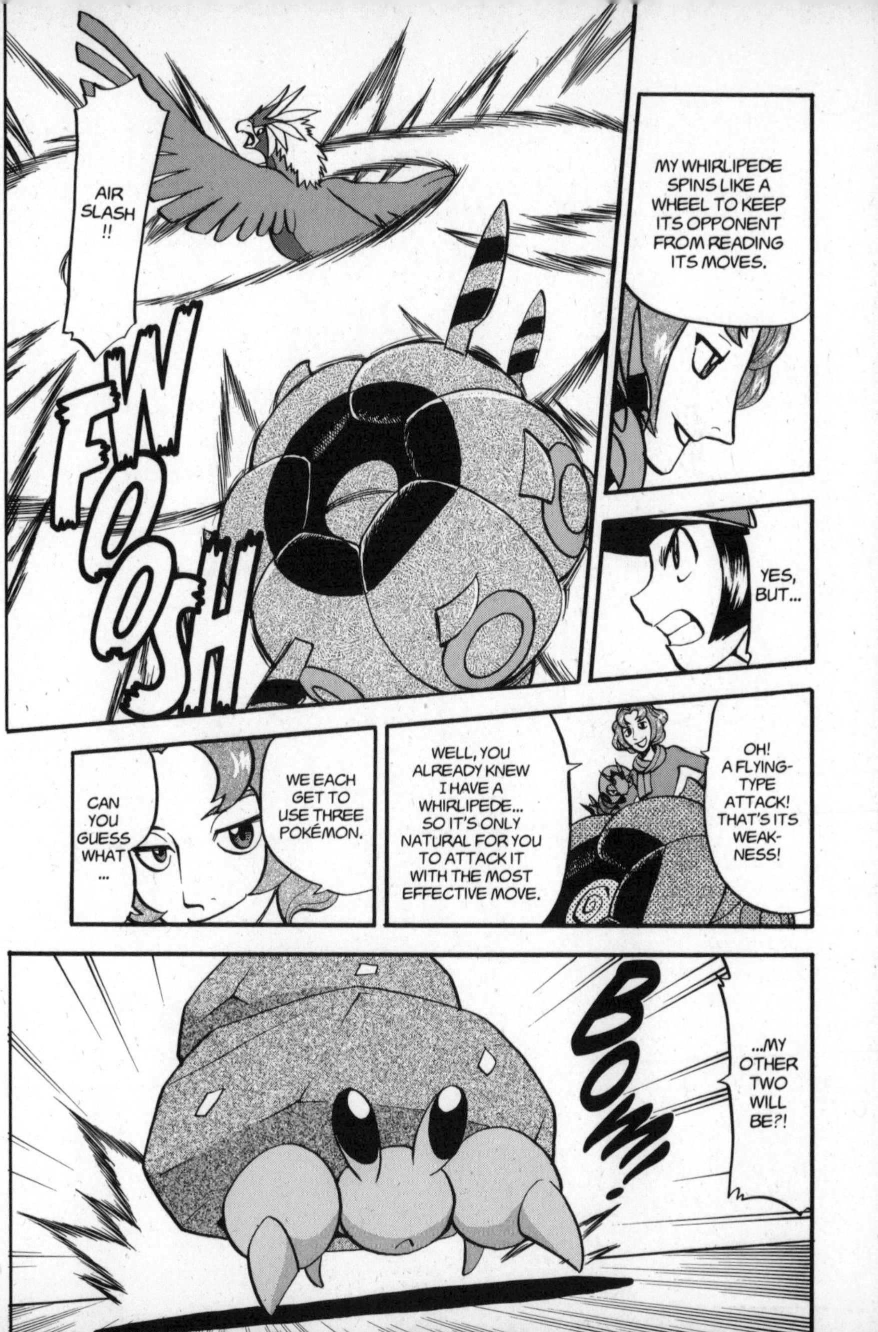
MY WHIRLIPEDE SPINS LIKE A WHEEL TO KEEP ITS OPPONENT FROM READING ITS MOVES.
AIR SLASH !!
FWOOOSH
YES, BUT...
OH! A FLYING-TYPE ATTACK! THAT'S ITS WEAK-NESS!
WELL, YOU ALREADY KNEW I HAVE A WHIRLIPEDE... SO IT'S ONLY NATURAL FOR YOU TO ATTACK IT WITH THE MOST EFFECTIVE MOVE.
WE EACH GET TO USE THREE POKÉMON.
CAN YOU GUESS WHAT ...
...MY OTHER TWO WILL BE?!
BOOM!!

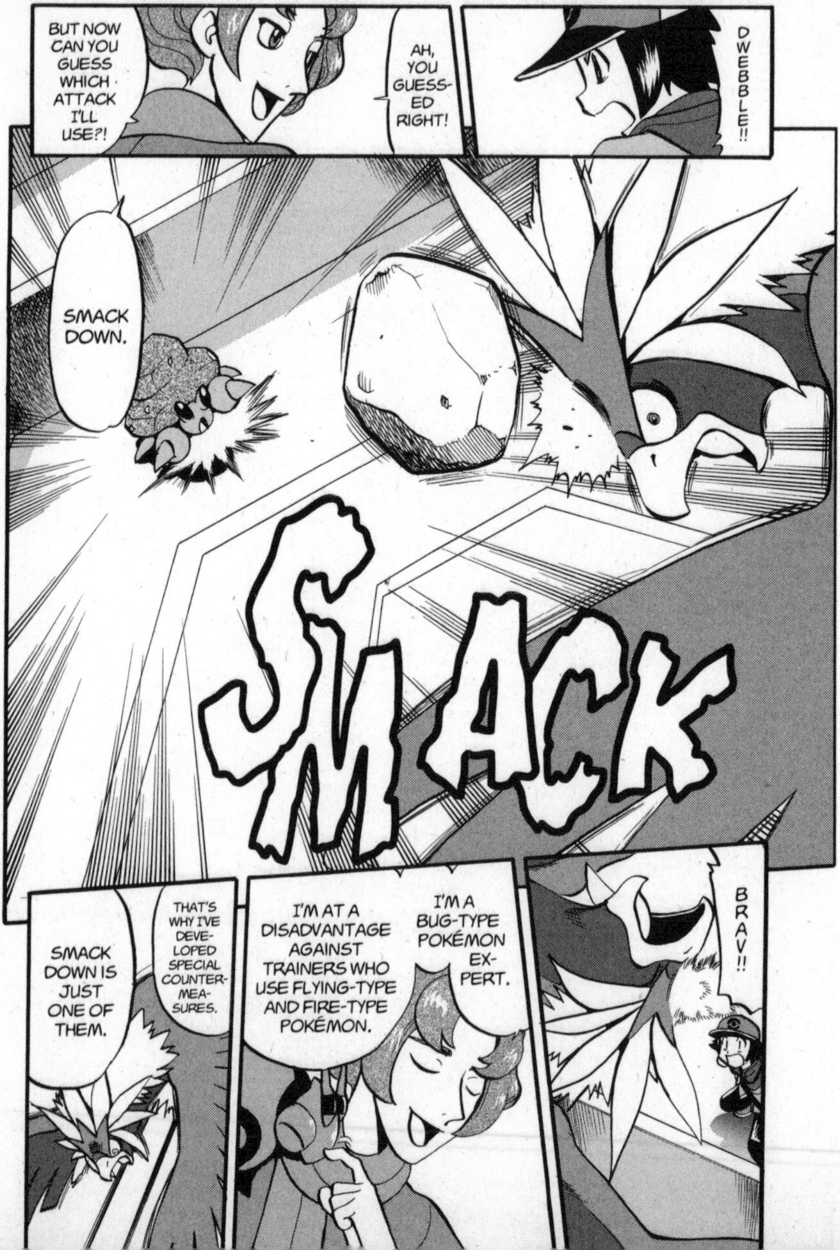
BUT NOW CAN YOU GUESS WHICH ATTACK I'LL USE?!
AH, YOU GUESS-ED RIGHT!
DWEBBLE!!
SMACK DOWN.
SMACK
I'M A BUG-TYPE POKÉMON EX-PERT.
I'M AT A DISADVANTAGE AGAINST TRAINERS WHO USE FLYING-TYPE AND FIRE-TYPE POKÉMON.
THAT'S WHY I'VE DEVE-LOPED SPECIAL COUNTER-MEA-SURES.
SMACK DOWN IS JUST ONE OF THEM.
BRAV!!

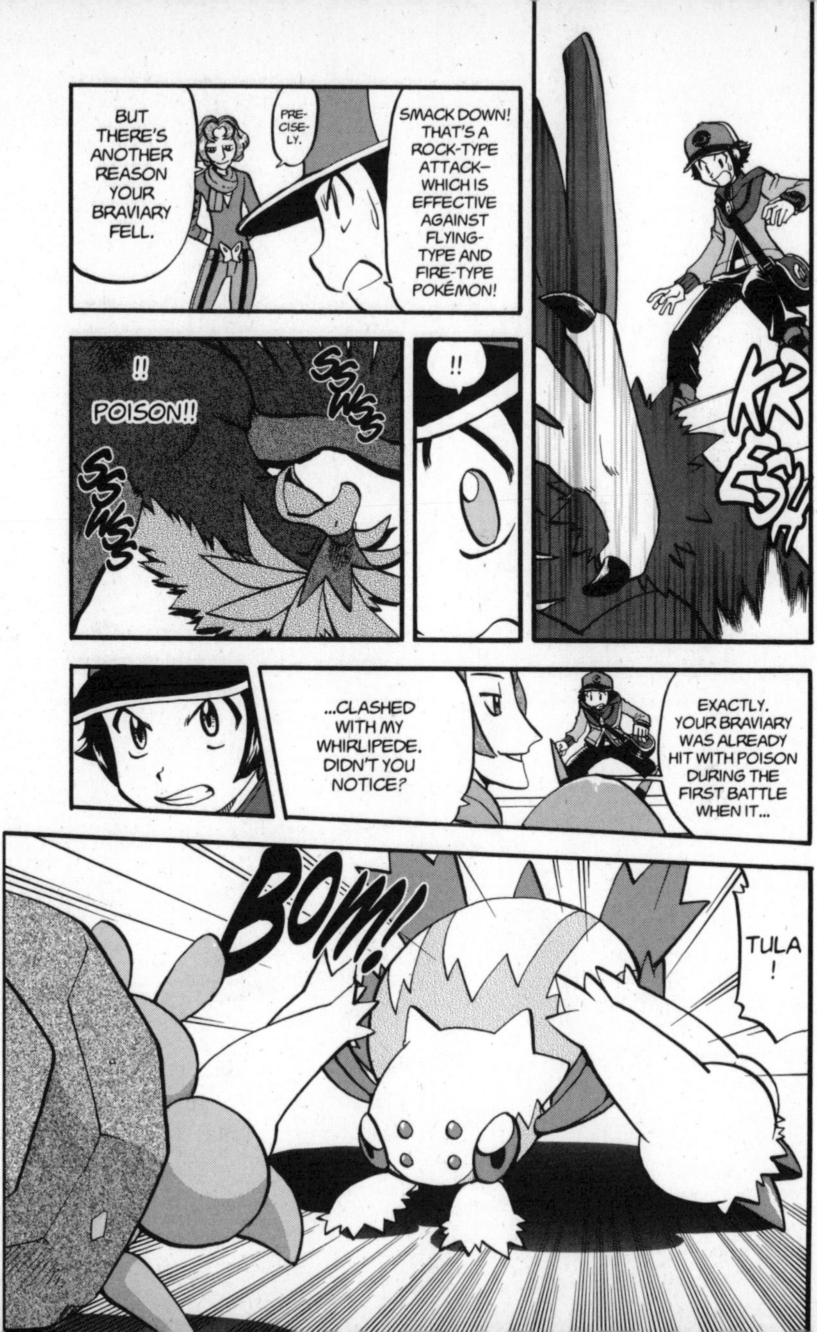
KRESH!!
SMACK DOWN! THAT'S A ROCK-TYPE ATTACK—WHICH IS EFFECTIVE AGAINST FLYING-TYPE AND FIRE-TYPE POKÉMON!
PRE-CISE-LY.
BUT THERE'S ANOTHER REASON YOUR BRAVIARY FELL.
!!
!!
POISON!!
SSWSS
SSWSS
EXACTLY. YOUR BRAVIARY WAS ALREADY HIT WITH POISON DURING THE FIRST BATTLE WHEN IT...
...CLASHED WITH MY WHIRLIPEDE. DIDN'T YOU NOTICE?
BOM!
TULA!

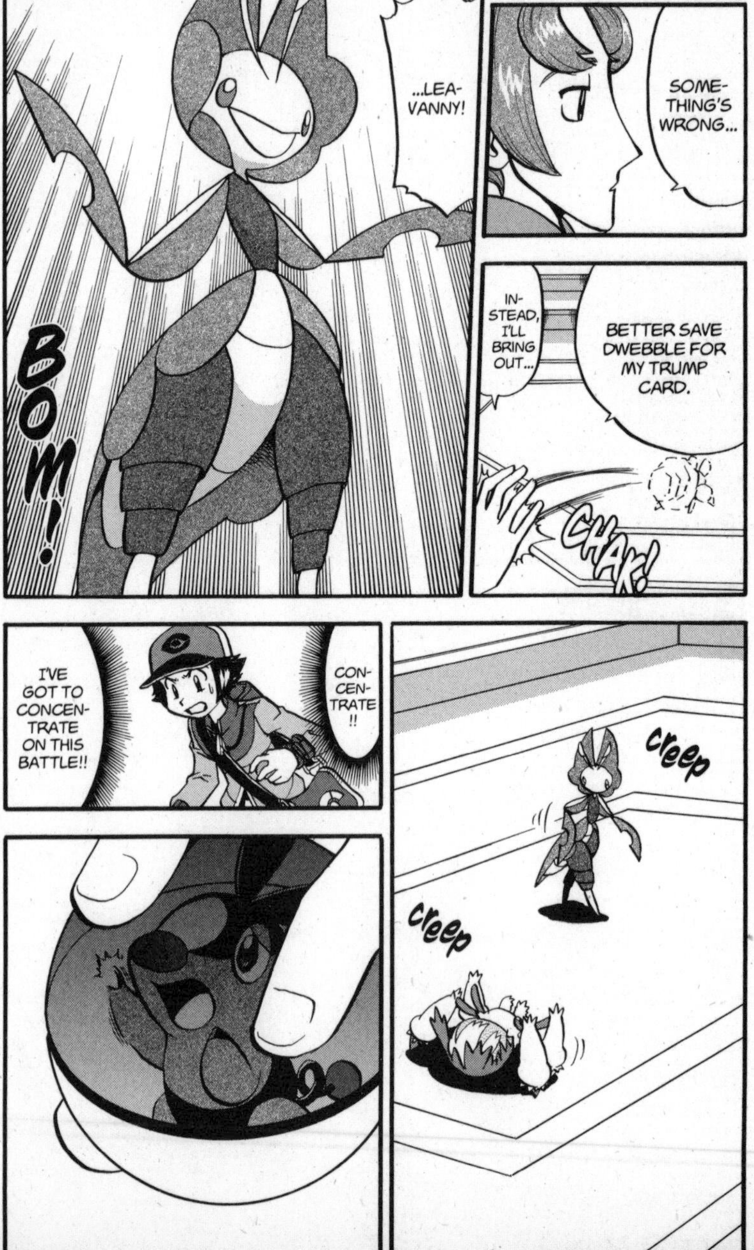
SOME-
THING'S
WRONG...
BETTER SAVE
DWEBBLE FOR
MY TRUMP
CARD.
IN-
STEAD,
I'LL
BRING
OUT...
CHAK!
...LEA-
VANNY!
BOOM!
creep
creep
CON-
CEN-
TRATE
!!
I'VE
GOT TO
CONCEN-
TRATE
ON THIS
BATTLE!!

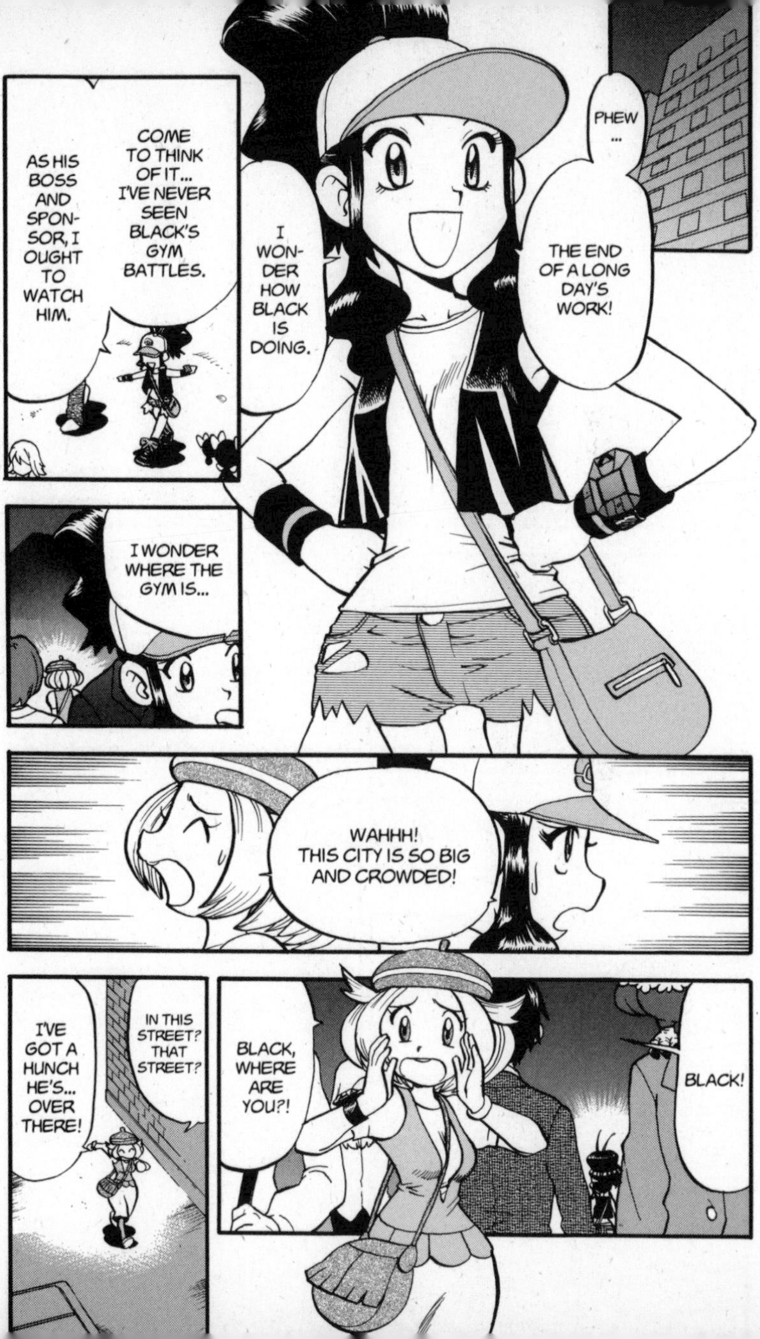
PHEW ...
THE END OF A LONG DAY'S WORK!
I WONDER HOW BLACK IS DOING.
COME TO THINK OF IT... I'VE NEVER SEEN BLACK'S GYM BATTLES.
AS HIS BOSS AND SPONSOR, I OUGHT TO WATCH HIM.
I WONDER WHERE THE GYM IS...
WAHHH! THIS CITY IS SO BIG AND CROWDED!
BLACK!
BLACK, WHERE ARE YOU?!
IN THIS STREET? THAT STREET?
I'VE GOT A HUNCH HE'S... OVER THERE!

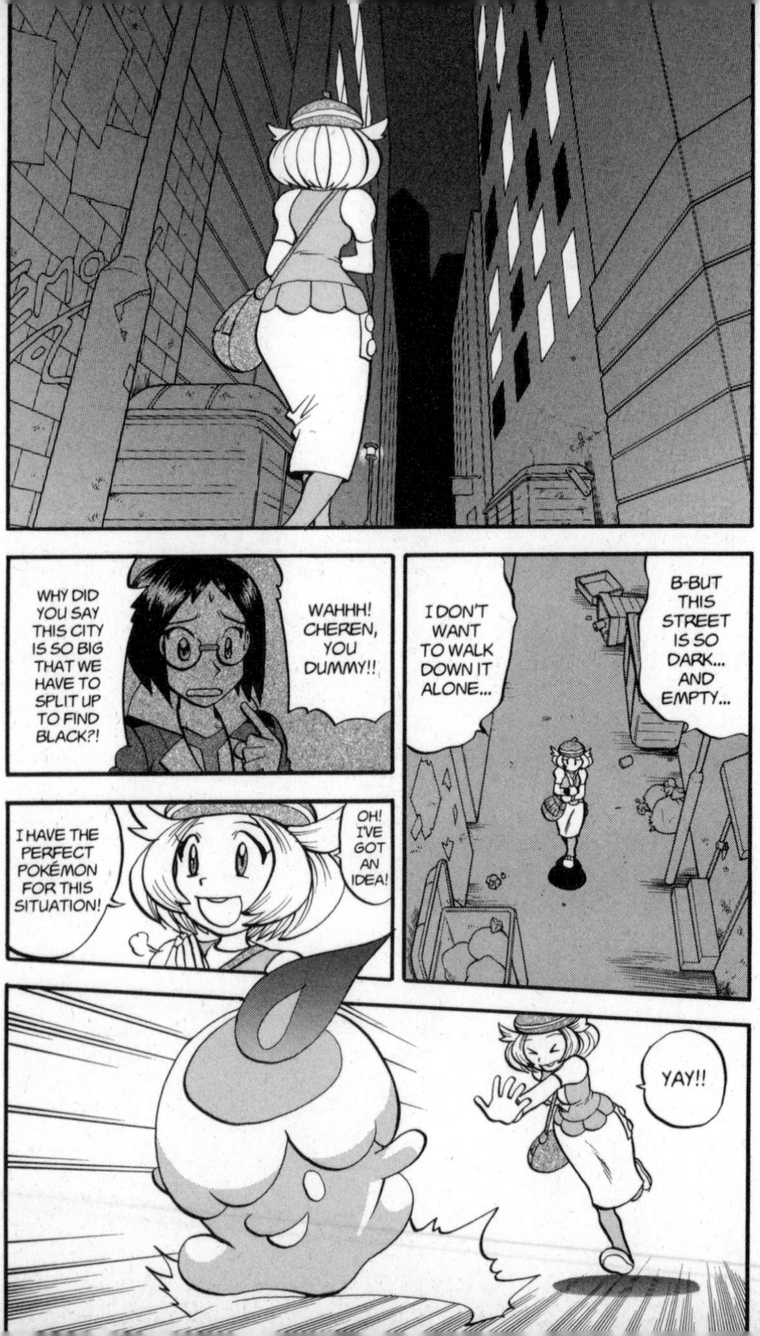
WHY DID YOU SAY THIS CITY IS SO BIG THAT WE HAVE TO SPLIT UP TO FIND BLACK?!
WAHHH! CHEREN, YOU DUMMY!!
I DON'T WANT TO WALK DOWN IT ALONE...
B-BUT THIS STREET IS SO DARK... AND EMPTY...
I HAVE THE PERFECT POKÉMON FOR THIS SITUATION!
OH! I'VE GOT AN IDEA!
YAY!!

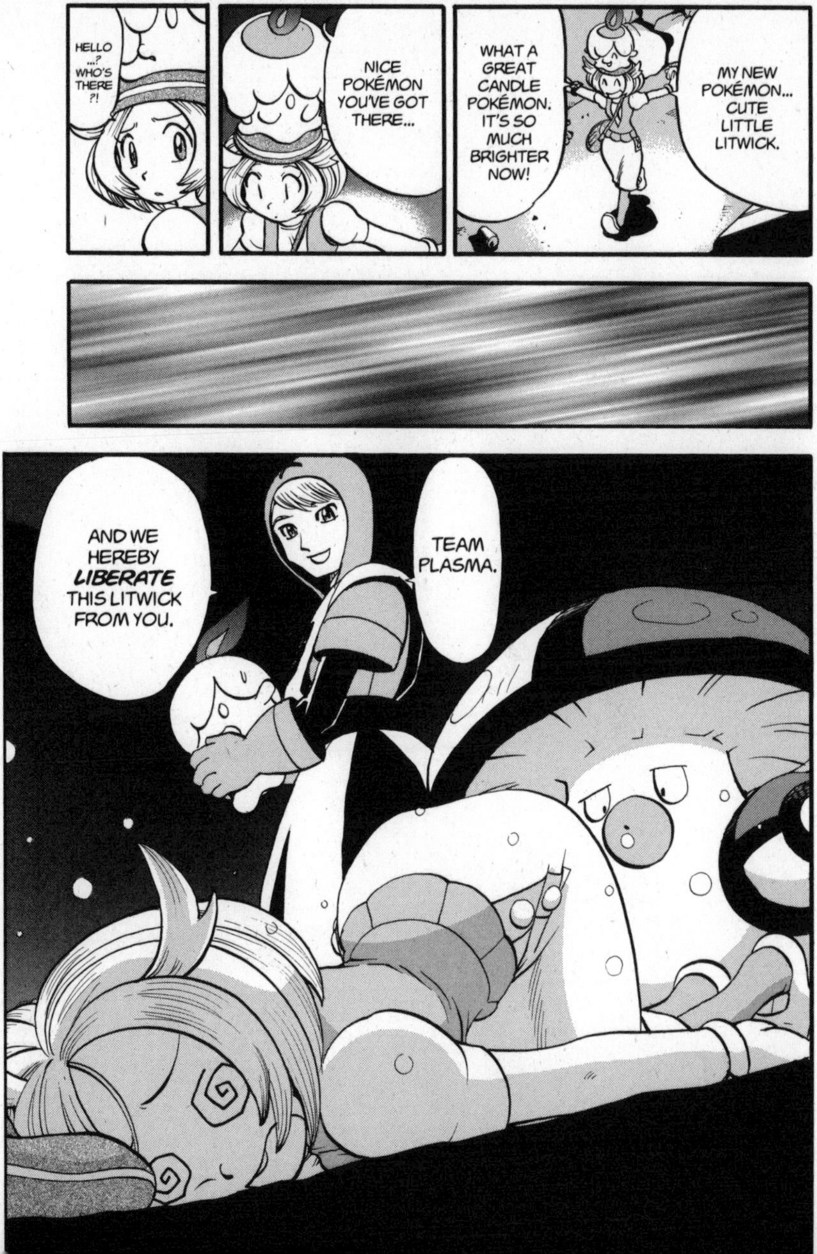
HELLO ...? WHO'S THERE ?!
NICE POKÉMON YOU'VE GOT THERE...
WHAT A GREAT CANDLE POKÉMON. IT'S SO MUCH BRIGHTER NOW!
MY NEW POKÉMON... CUTE LITTLE LITWICK.
TEAM PLASMA.
AND WE HEREBY ***LIBERATE*** THIS LITWICK FROM YOU.

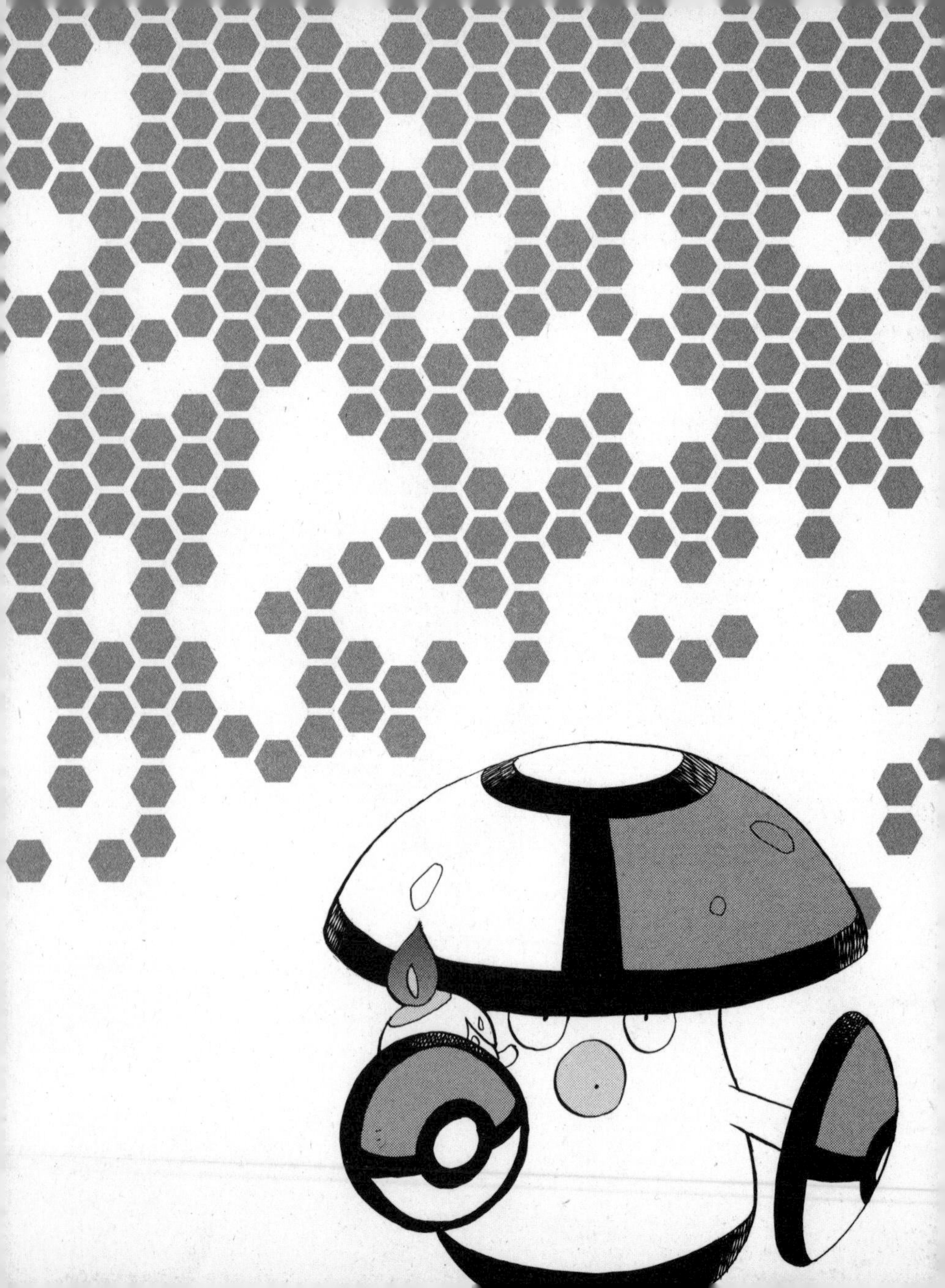

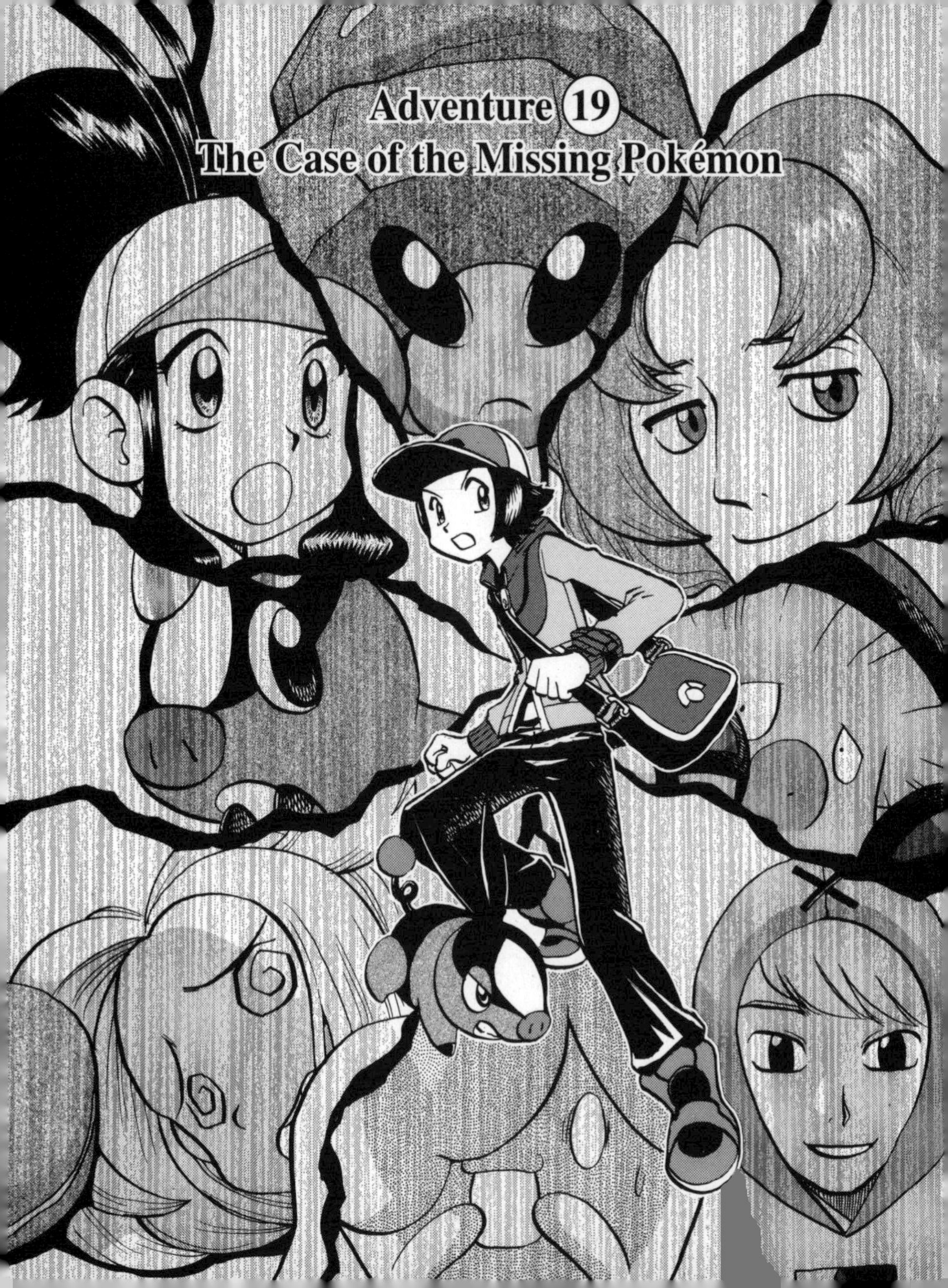
Adventure 19
The Case of the Missing Pokémon

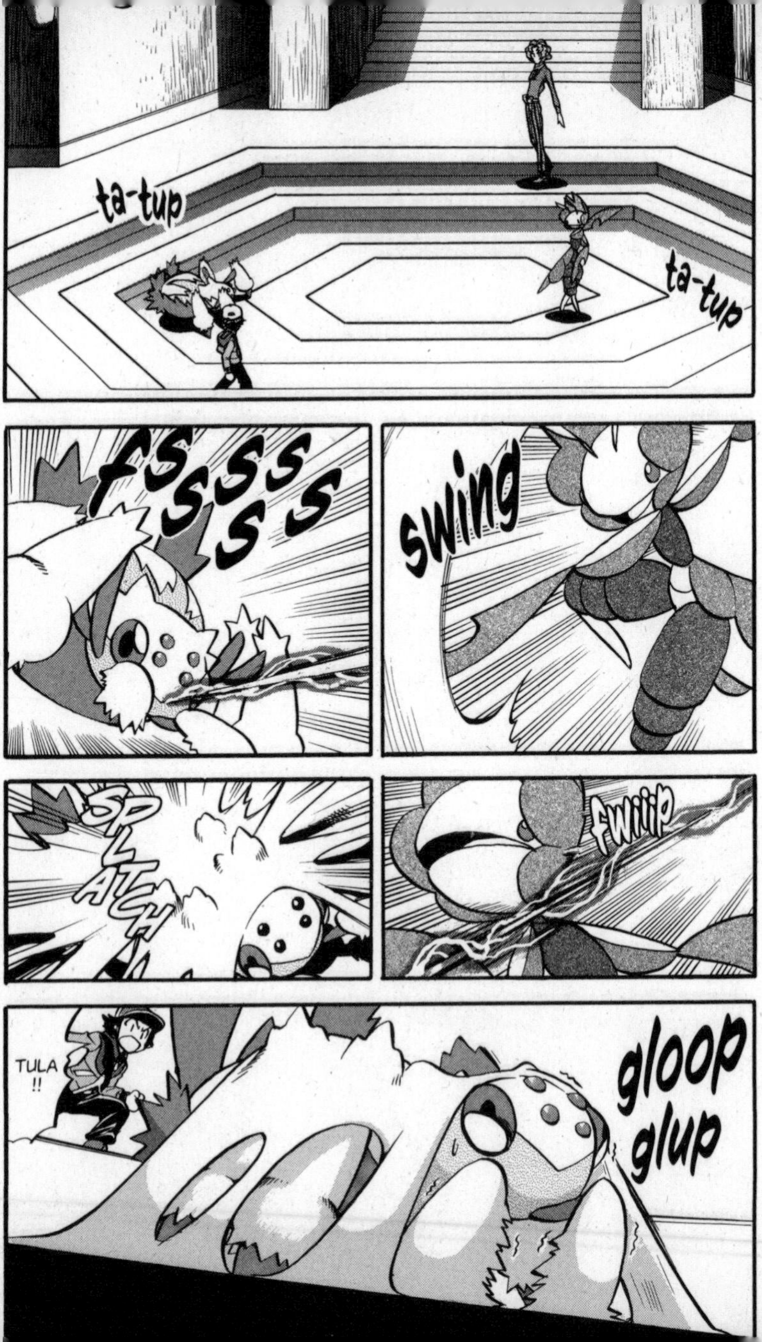
ta-tup
ta-tup
swing
fsssssss
fwiiip
SPLATCH
gloop
glup
TULA!!

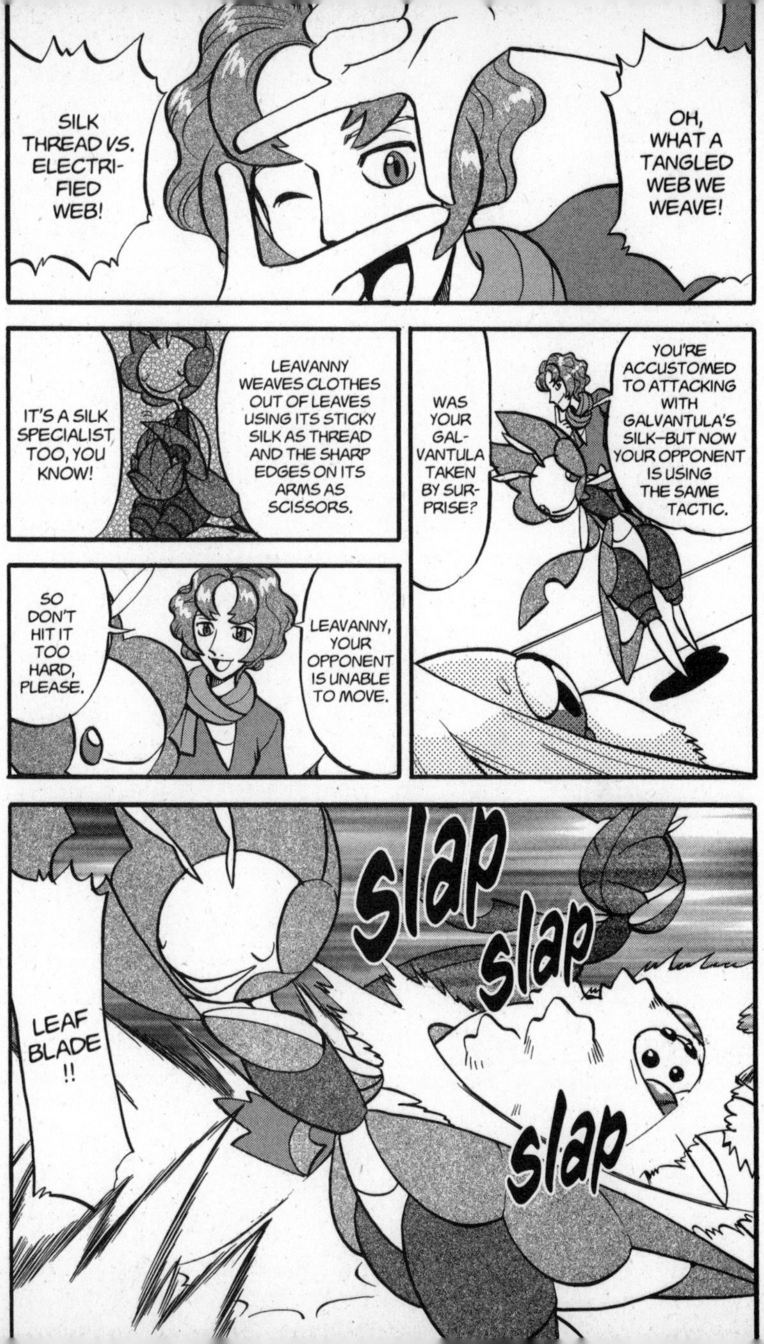
SILK THREAD VS. ELECTRI-FIED WEB!
OH, WHAT A TANGLED WEB WE WEAVE!
LEAVANNY WEAVES CLOTHES OUT OF LEAVES USING ITS STICKY SILK AS THREAD AND THE SHARP EDGES ON ITS ARMS AS SCISSORS.
IT'S A SILK SPECIALIST TOO, YOU KNOW!
WAS YOUR GAL-VANTULA TAKEN BY SUR-PRISE?
YOU'RE ACCUSTOMED TO ATTACKING WITH GALVANTULA'S SILK—BUT NOW YOUR OPPONENT IS USING THE SAME TACTIC.
LEAVANNY, YOUR OPPONENT IS UNABLE TO MOVE.
SO DON'T HIT IT TOO HARD, PLEASE.
LEAF BLADE !!
slap
slap
slap

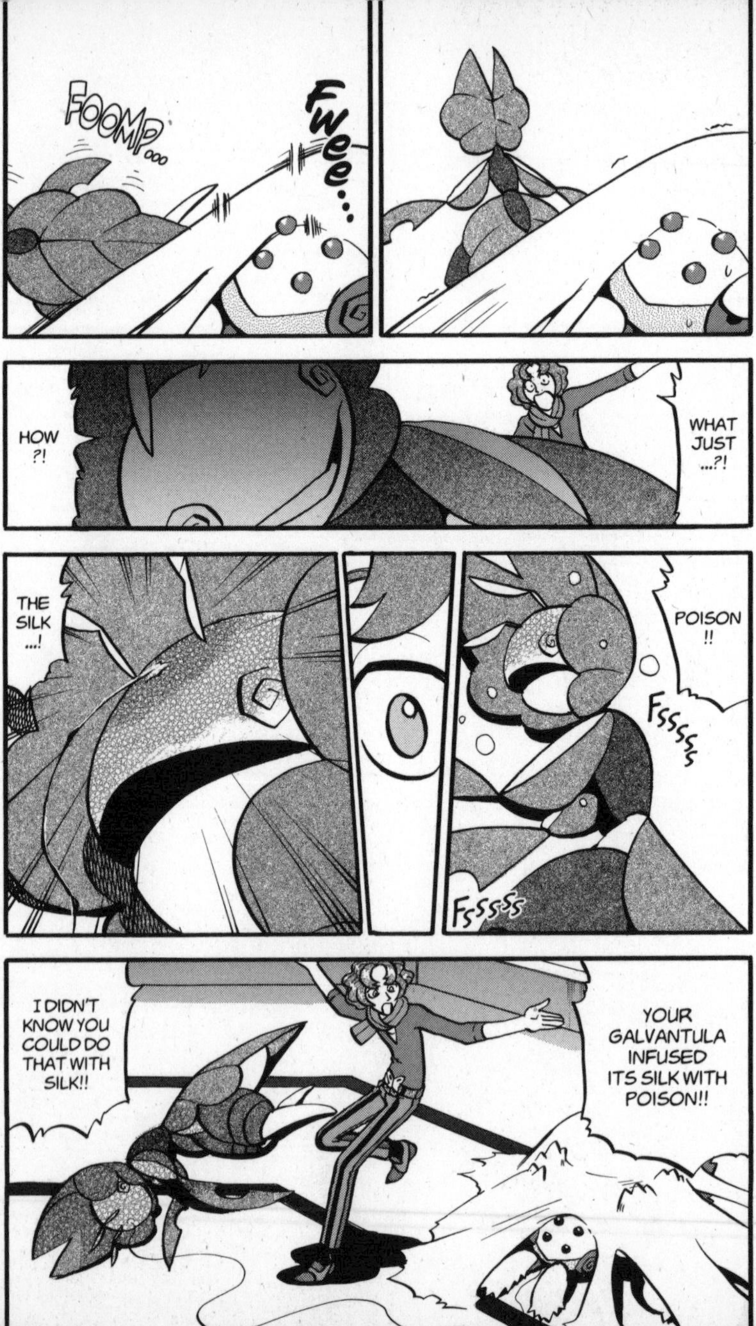
FOOMP...
Fwee...
HOW ?!
WHAT JUST ...?!
THE SILK ...!
POISON !!
Fsssss
Fsssss
I DIDN'T KNOW YOU COULD DO THAT WITH SILK!!
YOUR GALVANTULA INFUSED ITS SILK WITH POISON!!

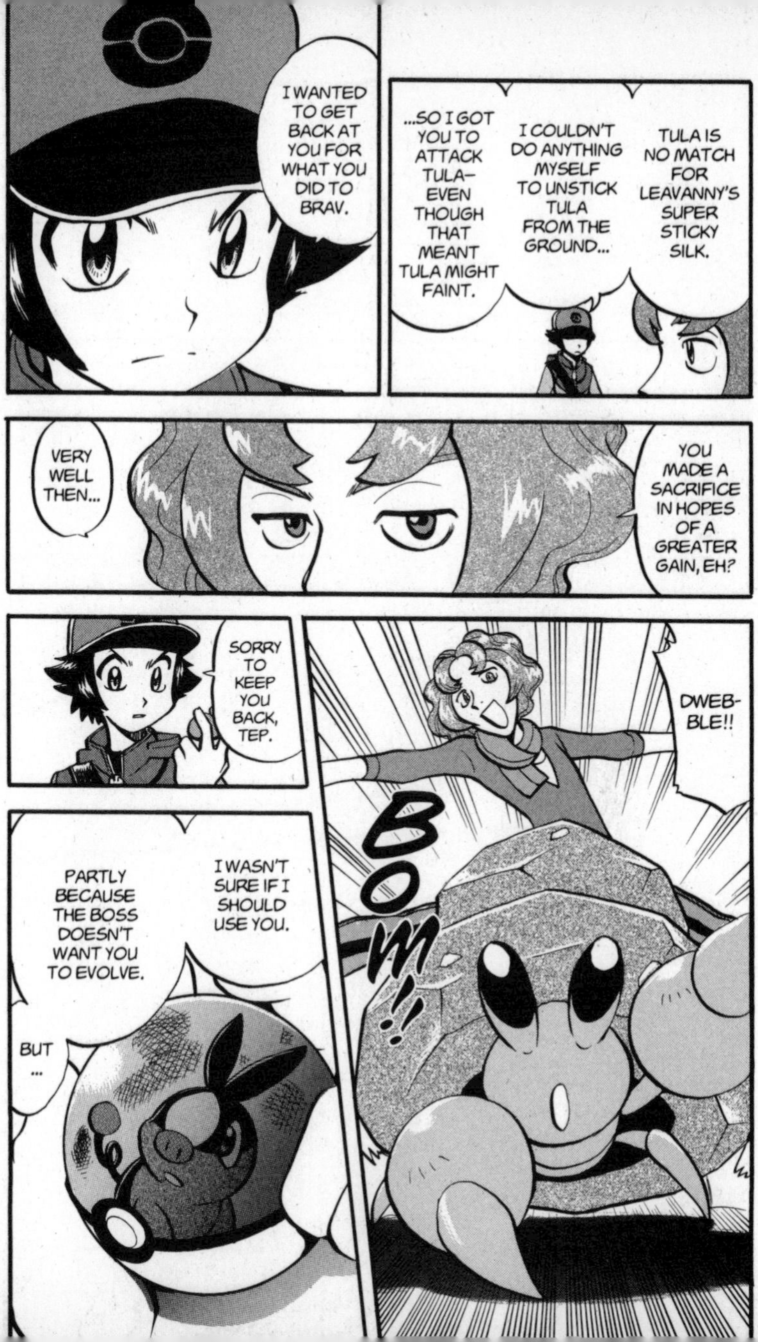
I WANTED TO GET BACK AT YOU FOR WHAT YOU DID TO BRAV.
TULA IS NO MATCH FOR LEAVANNY'S SUPER STICKY SILK.
I COULDN'T DO ANYTHING MYSELF TO UNSTICK TULA FROM THE GROUND...
...SO I GOT YOU TO ATTACK TULA—EVEN THOUGH THAT MEANT TULA MIGHT FAINT.
YOU MADE A SACRIFICE IN HOPES OF A GREATER GAIN, EH?
VERY WELL THEN...
SORRY TO KEEP YOU BACK, TEP.
I WASN'T SURE IF I SHOULD USE YOU.
PARTLY BECAUSE THE BOSS DOESN'T WANT YOU TO EVOLVE.
BUT ...
DWEBBLE!!
BOOM!!

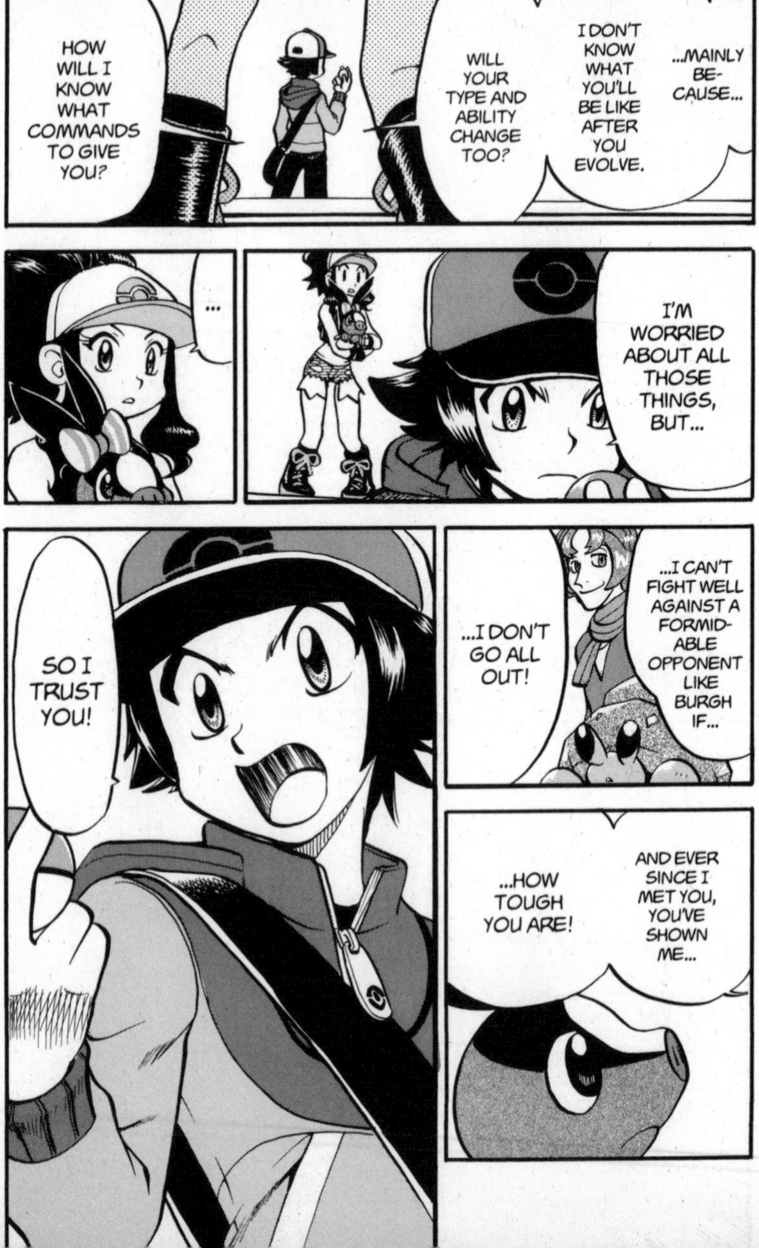
...MAINLY BE-CAUSE...
I DON'T KNOW WHAT YOU'LL BE LIKE AFTER YOU EVOLVE.
WILL YOUR TYPE AND ABILITY CHANGE TOO?
HOW WILL I KNOW WHAT COMMANDS TO GIVE YOU?
I'M WORRIED ABOUT ALL THOSE THINGS, BUT...
...
...I CAN'T FIGHT WELL AGAINST A FORMID-ABLE OPPONENT LIKE BURGH IF...
...I DON'T GO ALL OUT!
AND EVER SINCE I MET YOU, YOU'VE SHOWN ME...
...HOW TOUGH YOU ARE!
SO I TRUST YOU!

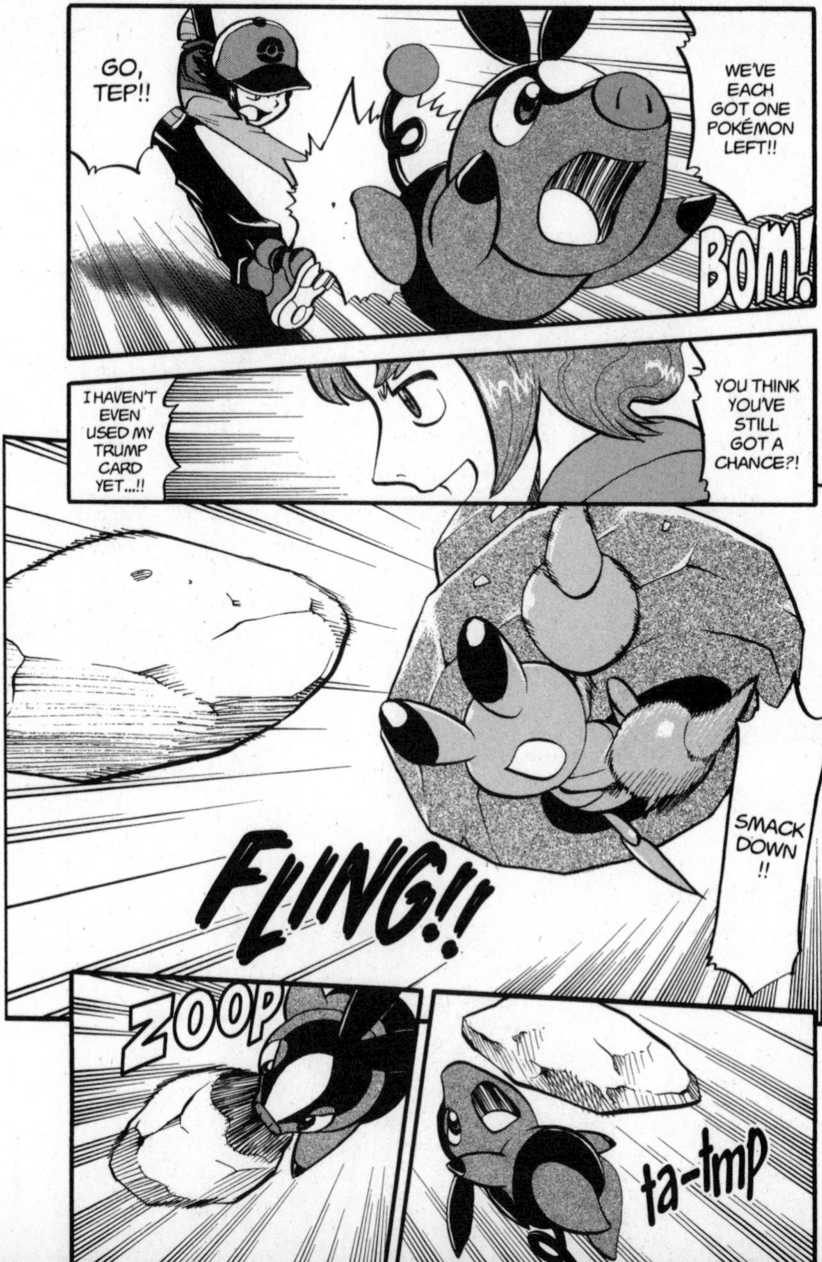
GO, TEP!!
WE'VE EACH GOT ONE POKÉMON LEFT!!
BOM!
I HAVEN'T EVEN USED MY TRUMP CARD YET...!!
YOU THINK YOU'VE STILL GOT A CHANCE?!
SMACK DOWN !!
FLING!!
ZOOP
ta-tmp

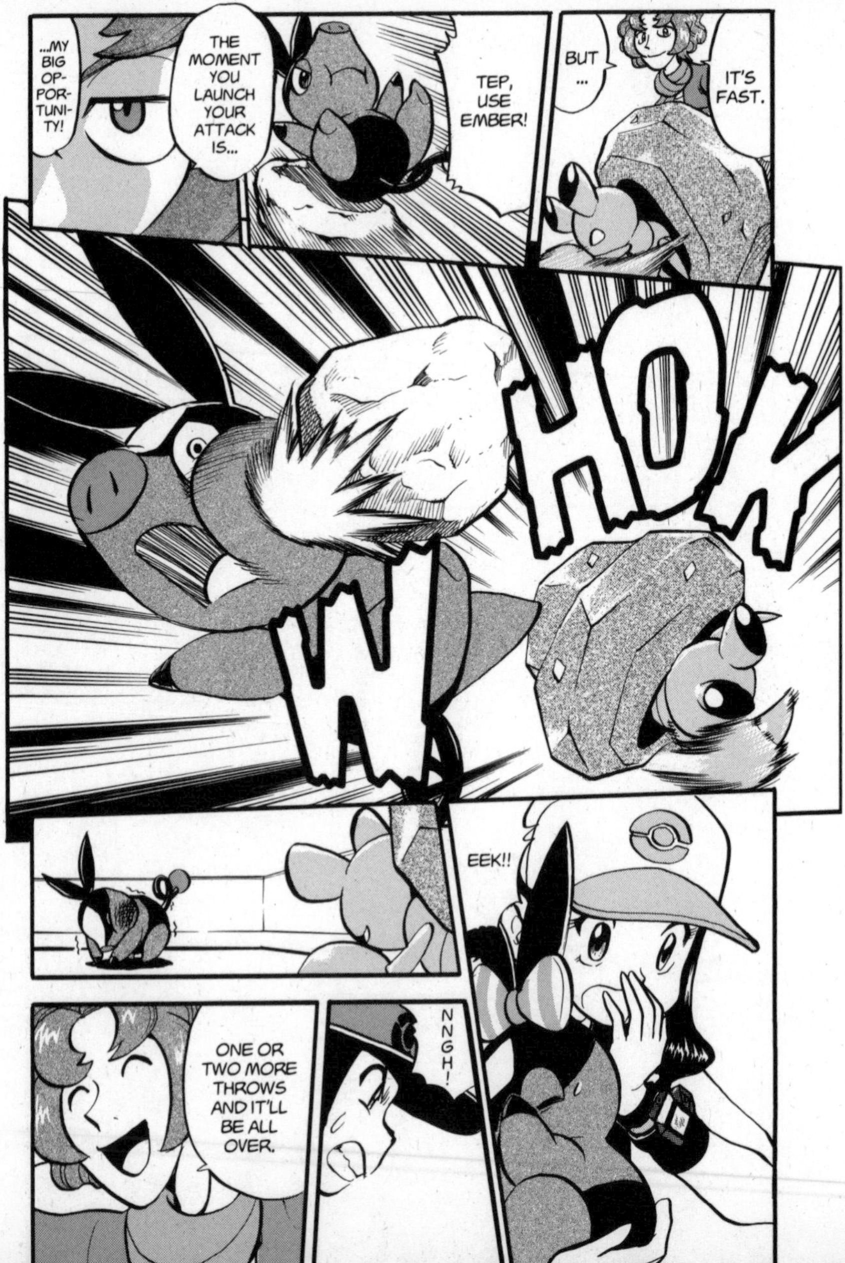
IT'S FAST.
BUT ...
TEP, USE EMBER!
THE MOMENT YOU LAUNCH YOUR ATTACK IS...
...MY BIG OP-POR-TUNI-TY!
WHOK
EEK!!
NNGH!
ONE OR TWO MORE THROWS AND IT'LL BE ALL OVER.

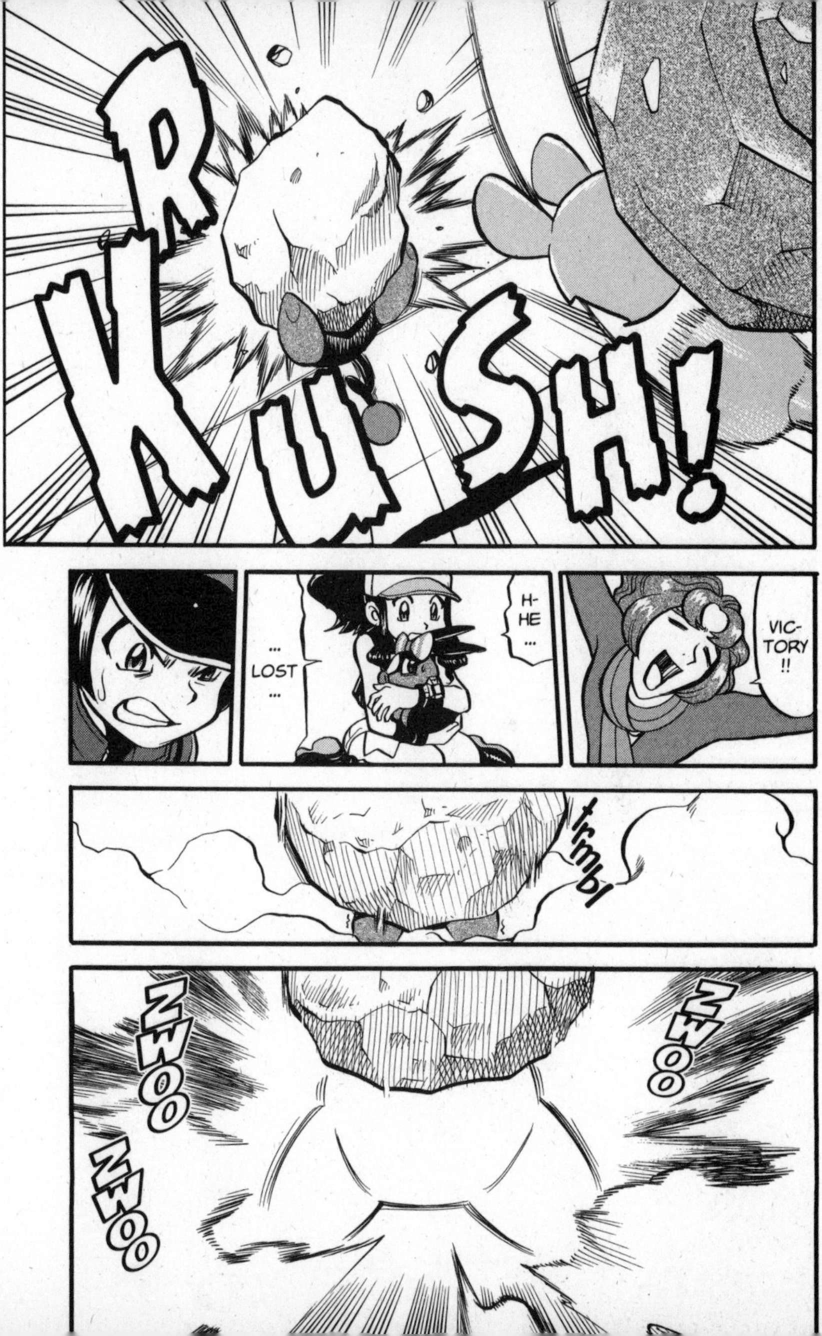
KRUSH!
H-
HE
...
...
LOST
...
VIC-
TORY
!!
trmbl
ZWOO
ZWOO
NWOO

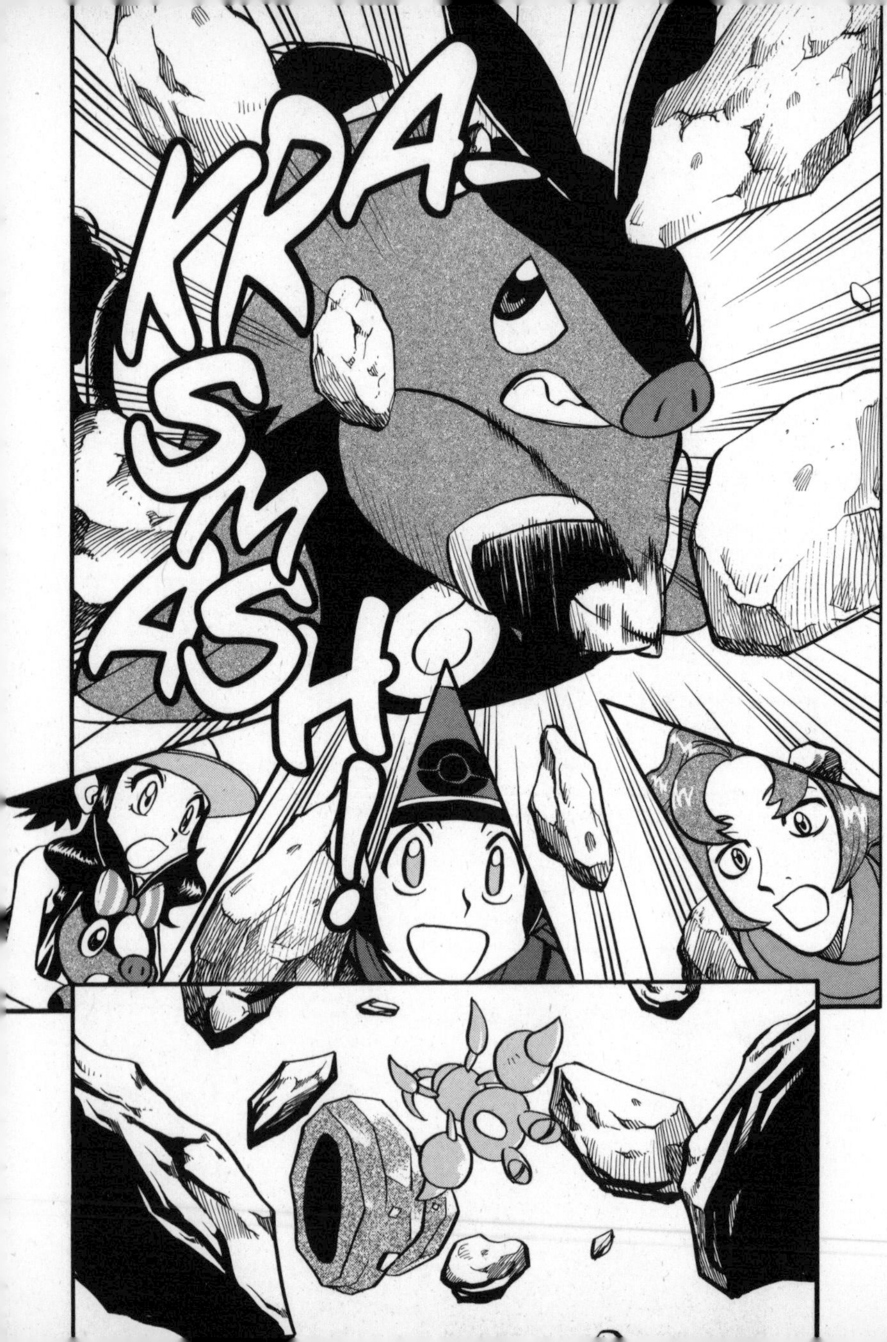
KRASMASH!

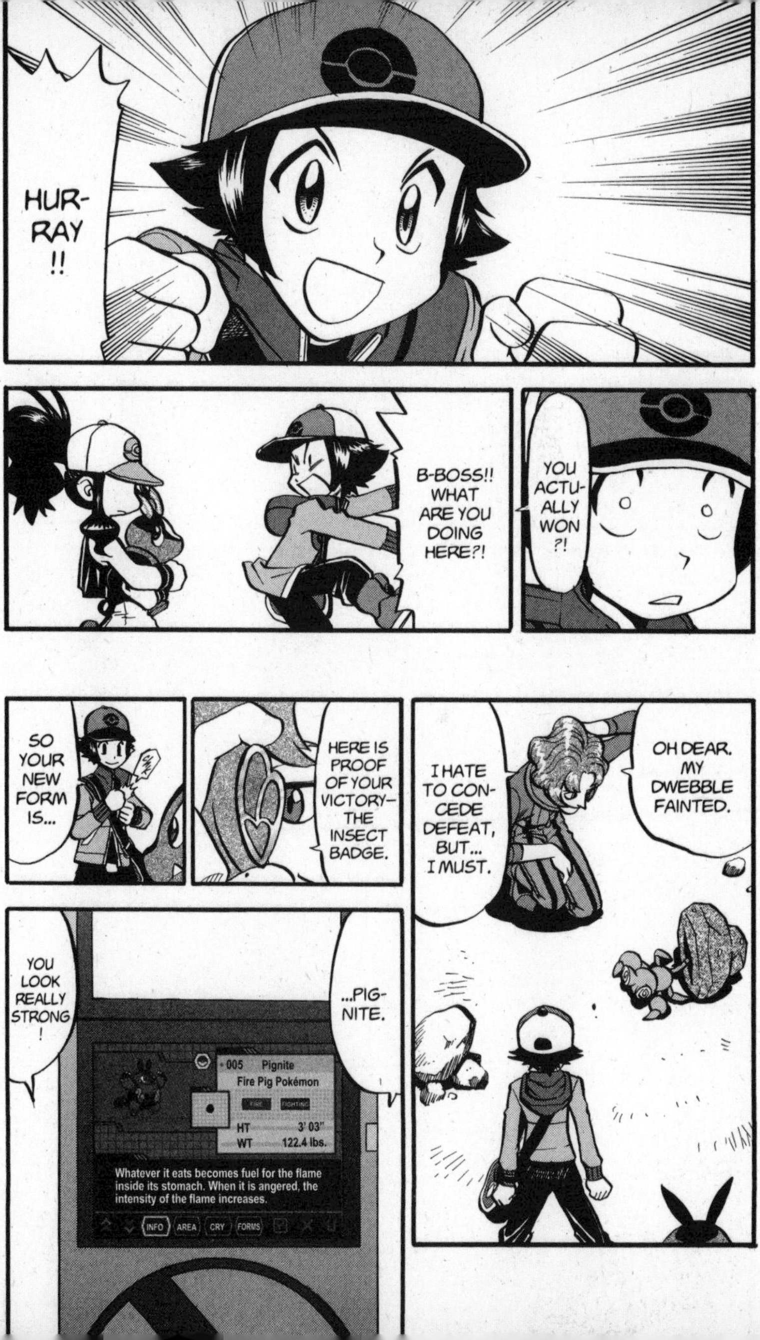
HUR-RAY!!
YOU ACTU-ALLY WON?!
B-BOSS!! WHAT ARE YOU DOING HERE?!
OH DEAR. MY DWEBBLE FAINTED.
I HATE TO CON-CEDE DEFEAT, BUT... I MUST.
HERE IS PROOF OF YOUR VICTORY—THE INSECT BADGE.
SO YOUR NEW FORM IS...
...PIG-NITE.
YOU LOOK REALLY STRONG!
005 Pignite
Fire Pig Pokémon
FIRE
FIGHTING
HT 3' 03"
WT 122.4 lbs.
Whatever it eats becomes fuel for the flame inside its stomach. When it is angered, the intensity of the flame increases.
INFO
AREA
CRY
FORMS

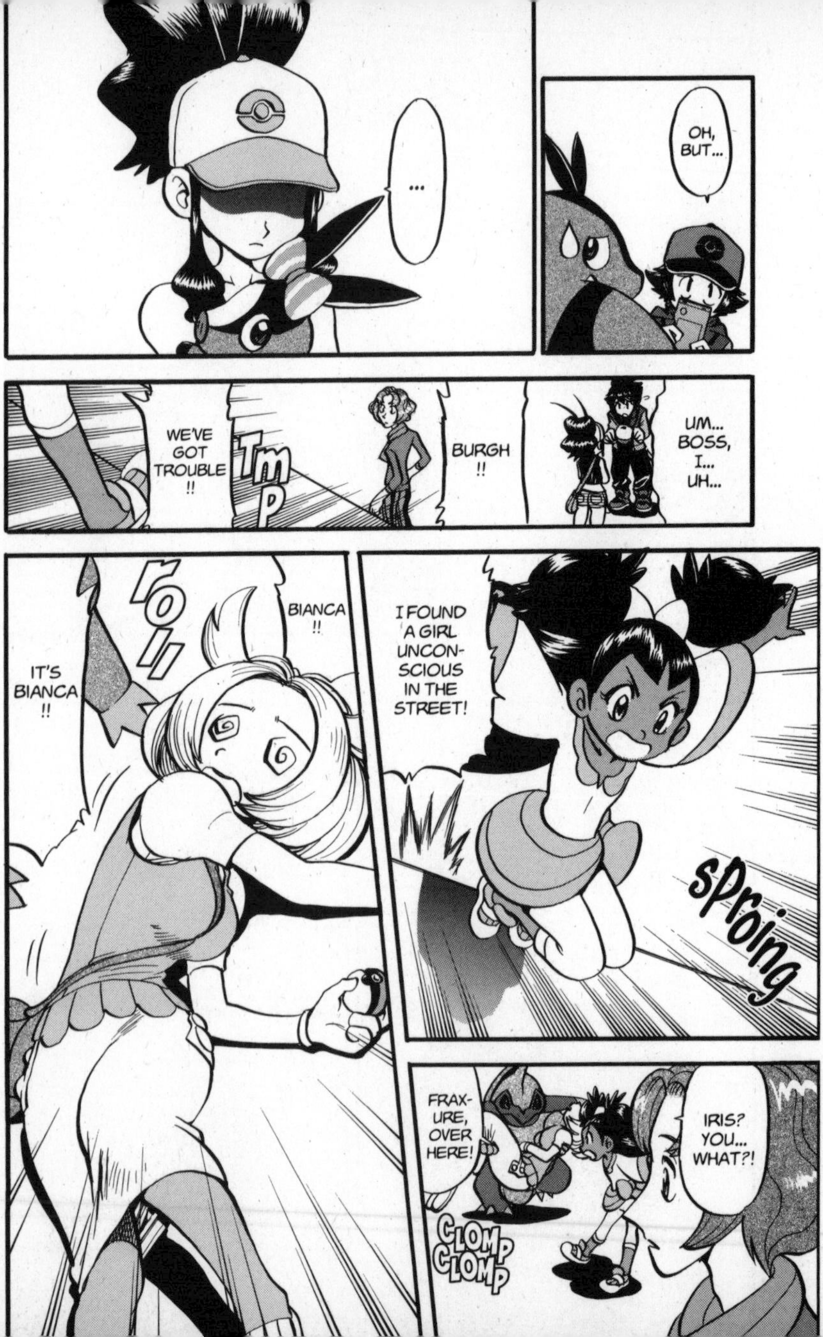
...
OH, BUT...
WE'VE GOT TROUBLE!!
TMP
BURGH!!
UM... BOSS, I... UH...
ROLL
IT'S BIANCA!!
BIANCA!!
I FOUND A GIRL UNCONSCIOUS IN THE STREET!
SPROING
FRAXURE, OVER HERE!
IRIS? YOU... WHAT?!
CLOMP CLOMP

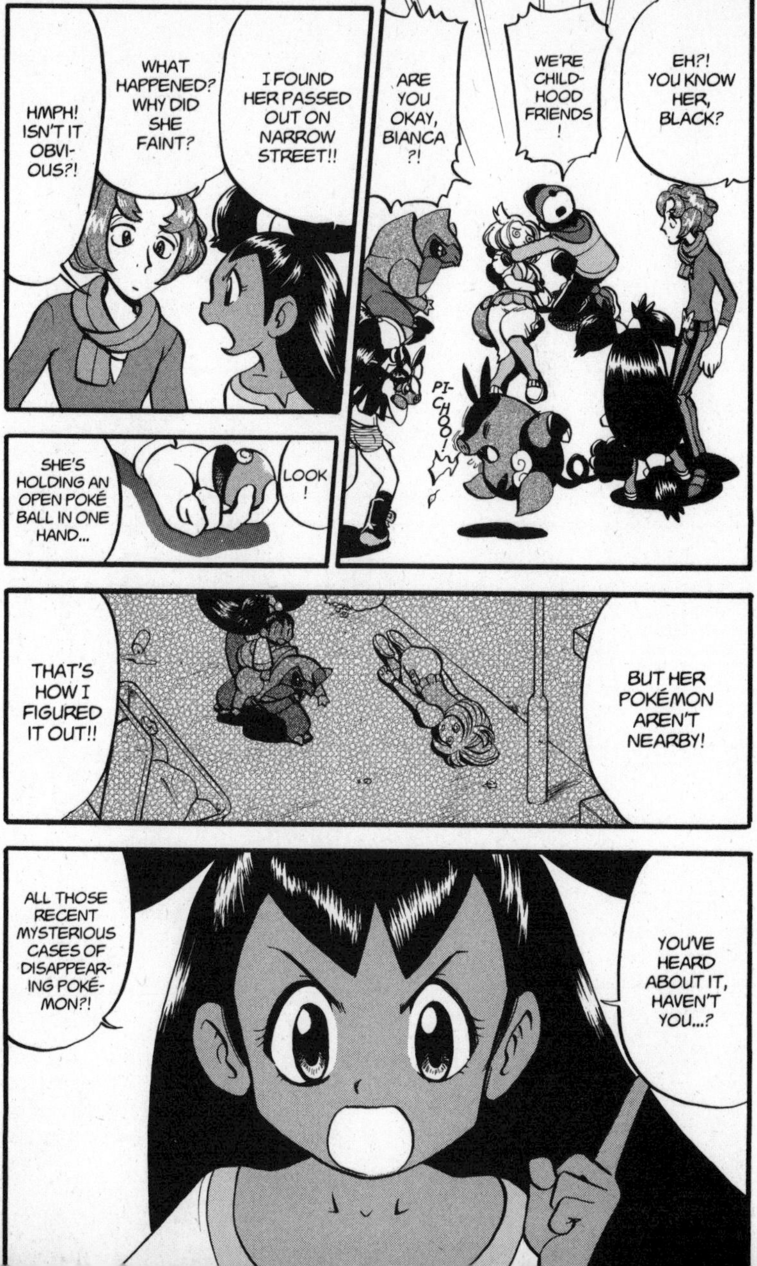

EH?! YOU KNOW HER, BLACK?
WE'RE CHILDHOOD FRIENDS!
ARE YOU OKAY, BIANCA?!
PI-CHOO!!
I FOUND HER PASSED OUT ON NARROW STREET!!
WHAT HAPPENED? WHY DID SHE FAINT?
HMPH! ISN'T IT OBVIOUS?!
LOOK!
SHE'S HOLDING AN OPEN POKÉ BALL IN ONE HAND...
BUT HER POKÉMON AREN'T NEARBY!
THAT'S HOW I FIGURED IT OUT!!
YOU'VE HEARD ABOUT IT, HAVEN'T YOU...?
ALL THOSE RECENT MYSTERIOUS CASES OF DISAPPEARING POKÉMON?!

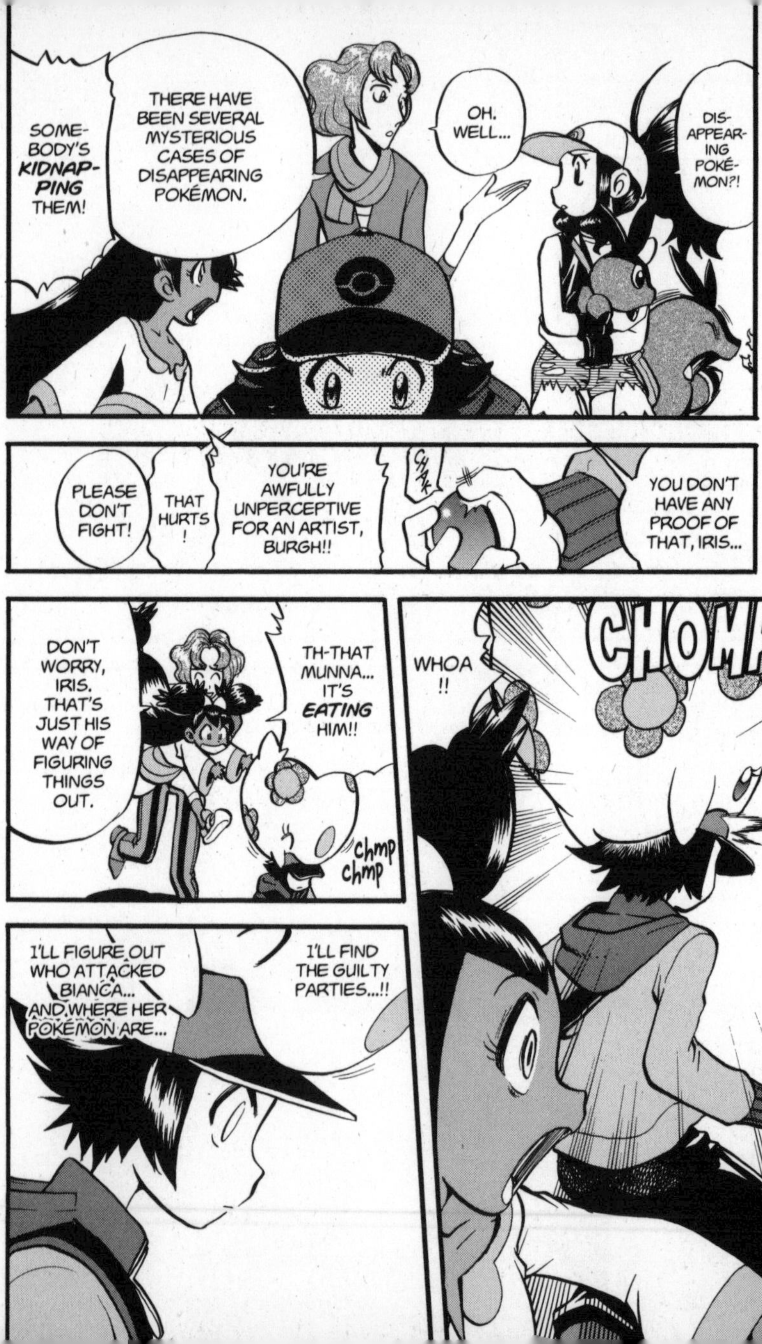
DIS-APPEARING POKÉMON?!
OH. WELL...
THERE HAVE BEEN SEVERAL MYSTERIOUS CASES OF DISAPPEARING POKÉMON.
SOME-BODY'S ***KIDNAPPING*** THEM!
YOU DON'T HAVE ANY PROOF OF THAT, IRIS...
CHAK
YOU'RE AWFULLY UNPERCEPTIVE FOR AN ARTIST, BURGH!!
THAT HURTS!
PLEASE DON'T FIGHT!
CHOMP
WHOA!!
TH-THAT MUNNA... IT'S ***EATING*** HIM!!
DON'T WORRY, IRIS. THAT'S JUST HIS WAY OF FIGURING THINGS OUT.
Chmp Chmp
I'LL FIND THE GUILTY PARTIES...!!
I'LL FIGURE OUT WHO ATTACKED BIANCA... AND WHERE HER POKÉMON ARE...

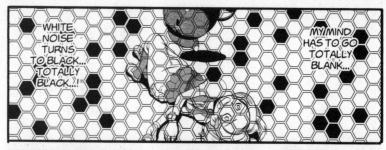

MY MIND HAS TO GO TOTALLY BLANK...
WHITE NOISE TURNS TO BLACK... TOTALLY BLACK...!
BURGH, THIS GYM SMELLS REALLY STRONGLY OF HONEY, RIGHT?
un-chomp!
CORRECT! YOU DETECT THE SCENT OF MY ART INSTALLA-TION!
BUT... OUR NOSES CAN'T DISTINGUISH ANY LESS OBVIOUS SCENTS BECAUSE THE HONEY SMELL OVERWHELMS THEM...
...PIGNITE HAS A BETTER SENSE OF SMELL.
Pii...
Pii...

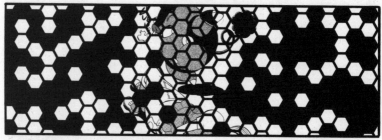

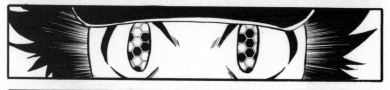

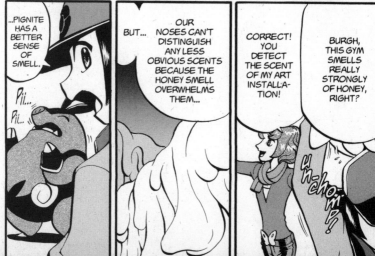

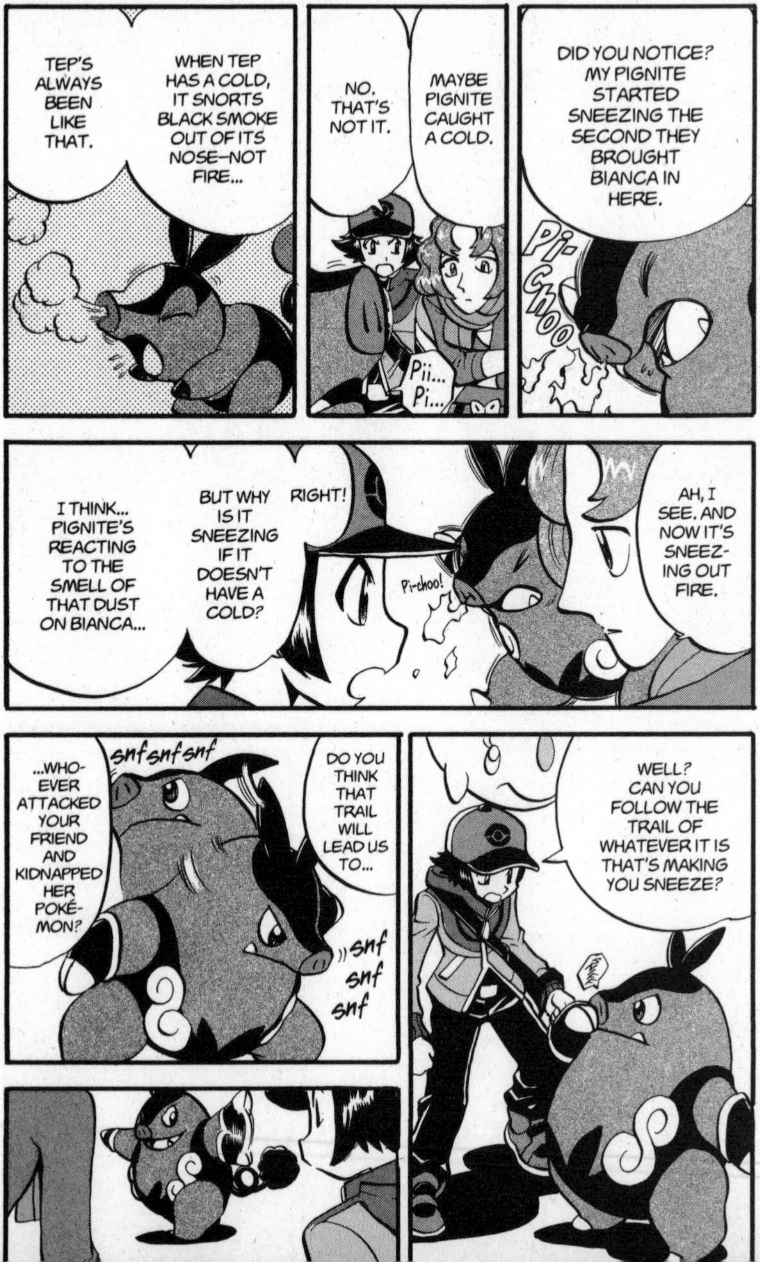

DID YOU NOTICE? MY PIGNITE STARTED SNEEZING THE SECOND THEY BROUGHT BIANCA IN HERE.
Pi-Chooo
MAYBE PIGNITE CAUGHT A COLD.
NO. THAT'S NOT IT.
Pii... Pi...
WHEN TEP HAS A COLD, IT SNORTS BLACK SMOKE OUT OF ITS NOSE–NOT FIRE...
TEP'S ALWAYS BEEN LIKE THAT.
AH, I SEE. AND NOW IT'S SNEEZ-ING OUT FIRE.
Pi-choo!
RIGHT!
BUT WHY IS IT SNEEZING IF IT DOESN'T HAVE A COLD?
I THINK... PIGNITE'S REACTING TO THE SMELL OF THAT DUST ON BIANCA...
WELL? CAN YOU FOLLOW THE TRAIL OF WHATEVER IT IS THAT'S MAKING YOU SNEEZE?
DO YOU THINK THAT TRAIL WILL LEAD US TO...
...WHO-EVER ATTACKED YOUR FRIEND AND KIDNAPPED HER POKÉ-MON?
snf snf snf
snf snf snf

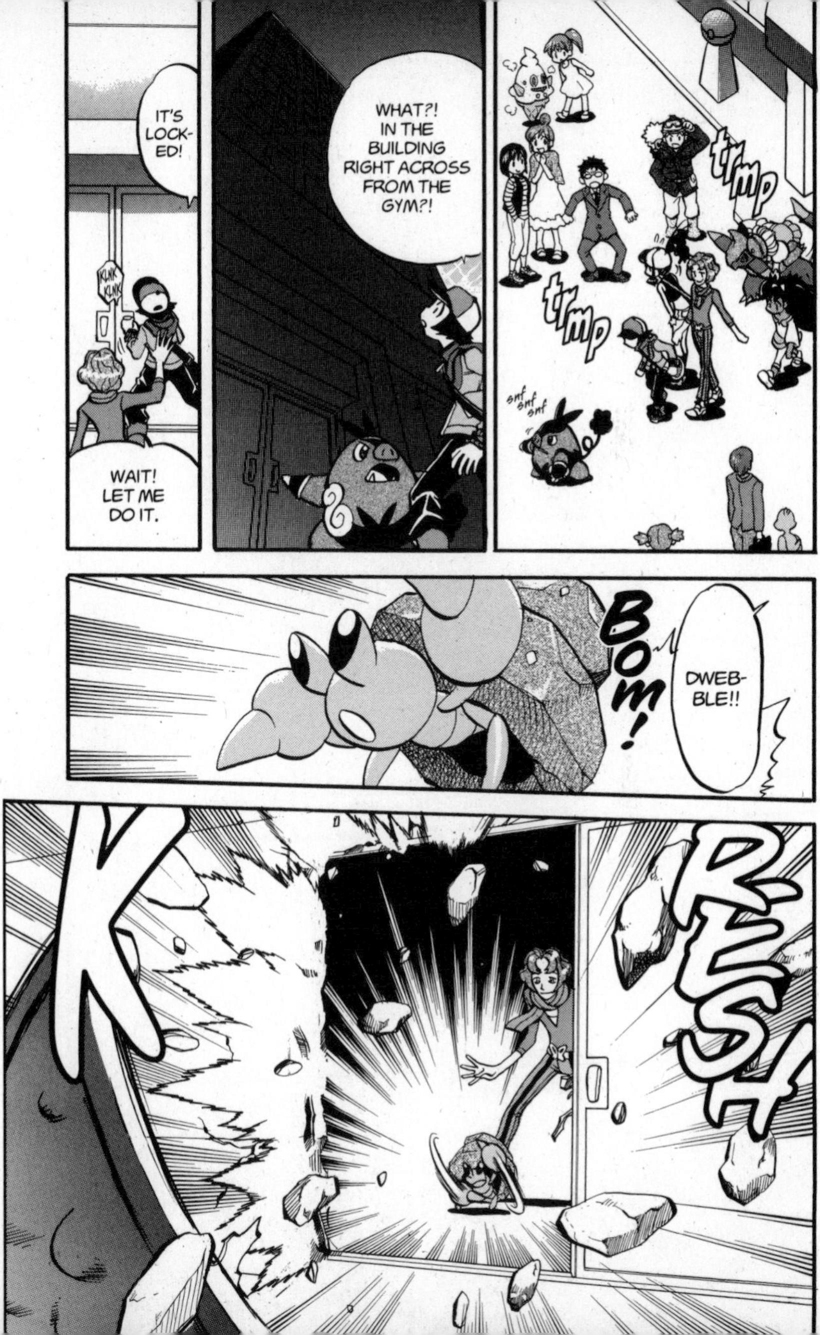

IT'S LOCK-ED!
KLNK KLNK
WAIT! LET ME DO IT.
WHAT?! IN THE BUILDING RIGHT ACROSS FROM THE GYM?!
trmp
trmp
snf snf snf
BOM!
DWEB-BLE!!
KRESH

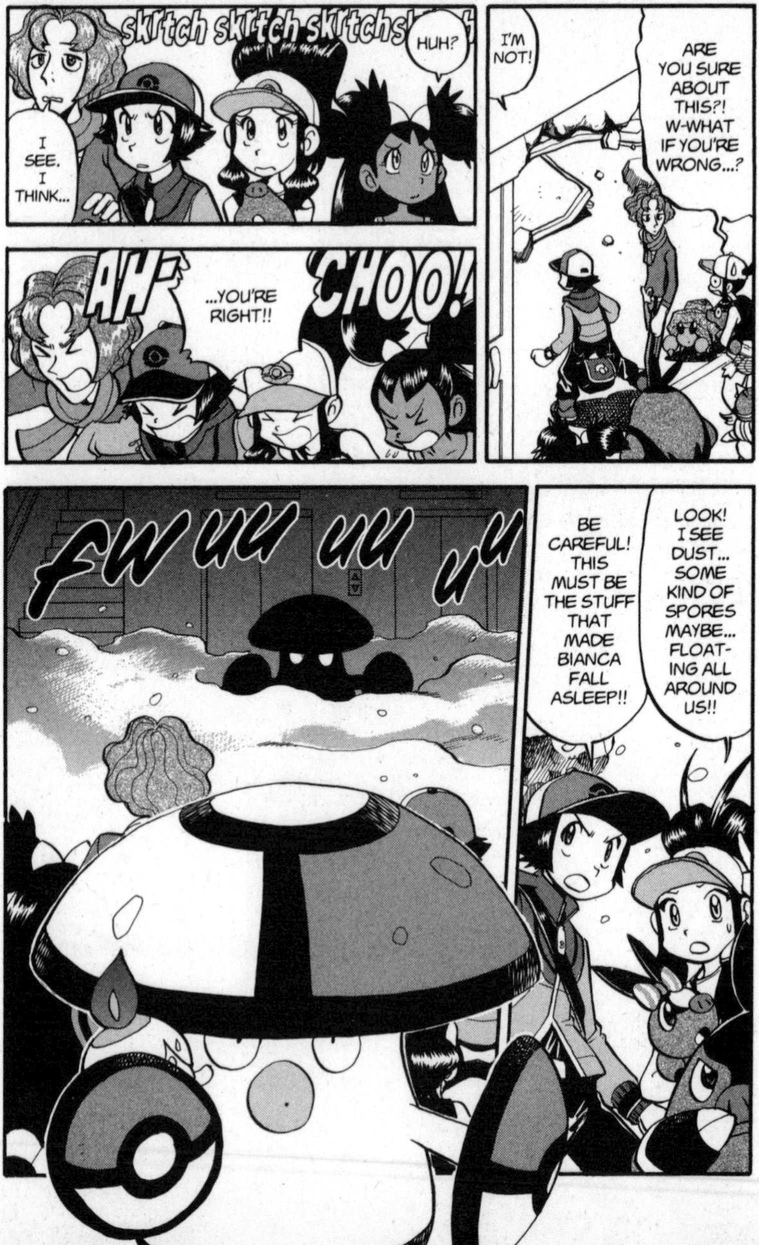
skritch skritch skritchskritch
HUH?
I SEE. I THINK...
I'M NOT!
ARE YOU SURE ABOUT THIS?! W-WHAT IF YOU'RE WRONG...?
AH-
...YOU'RE RIGHT!!
CHOO!!
FWUUU UUU UU
LOOK! I SEE DUST... SOME KIND OF SPORES MAYBE... FLOAT-ING ALL AROUND US!!
BE CAREFUL! THIS MUST BE THE STUFF THAT MADE BIANCA FALL ASLEEP!!

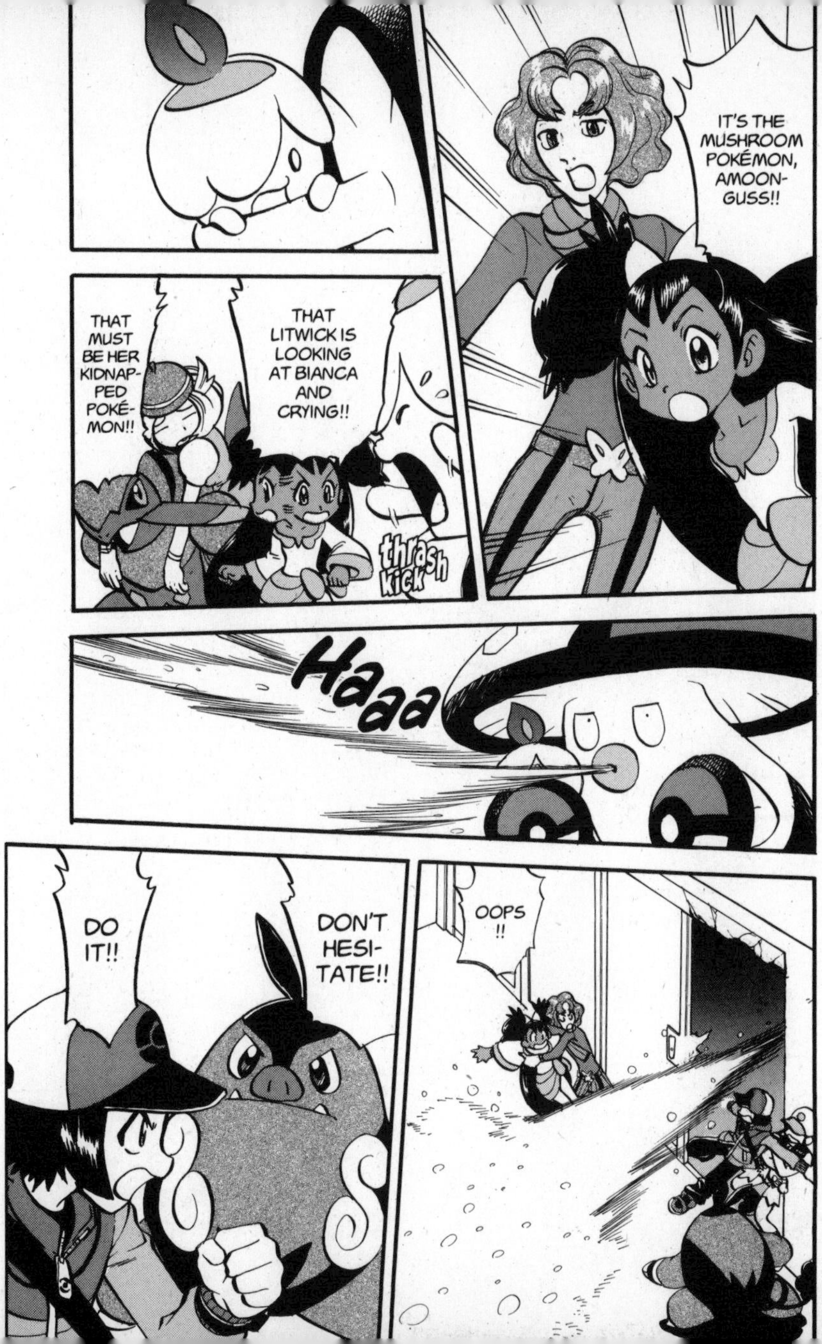
IT'S THE MUSHROOM POKÉMON, AMOONGUSS!!
THAT LITWICK IS LOOKING AT BIANCA AND CRYING!!
THAT MUST BE HER KIDNAPPED POKÉMON!!
thrash
kick
Haaa
DO IT!!
DON'T HESITATE!!
OOPS!!

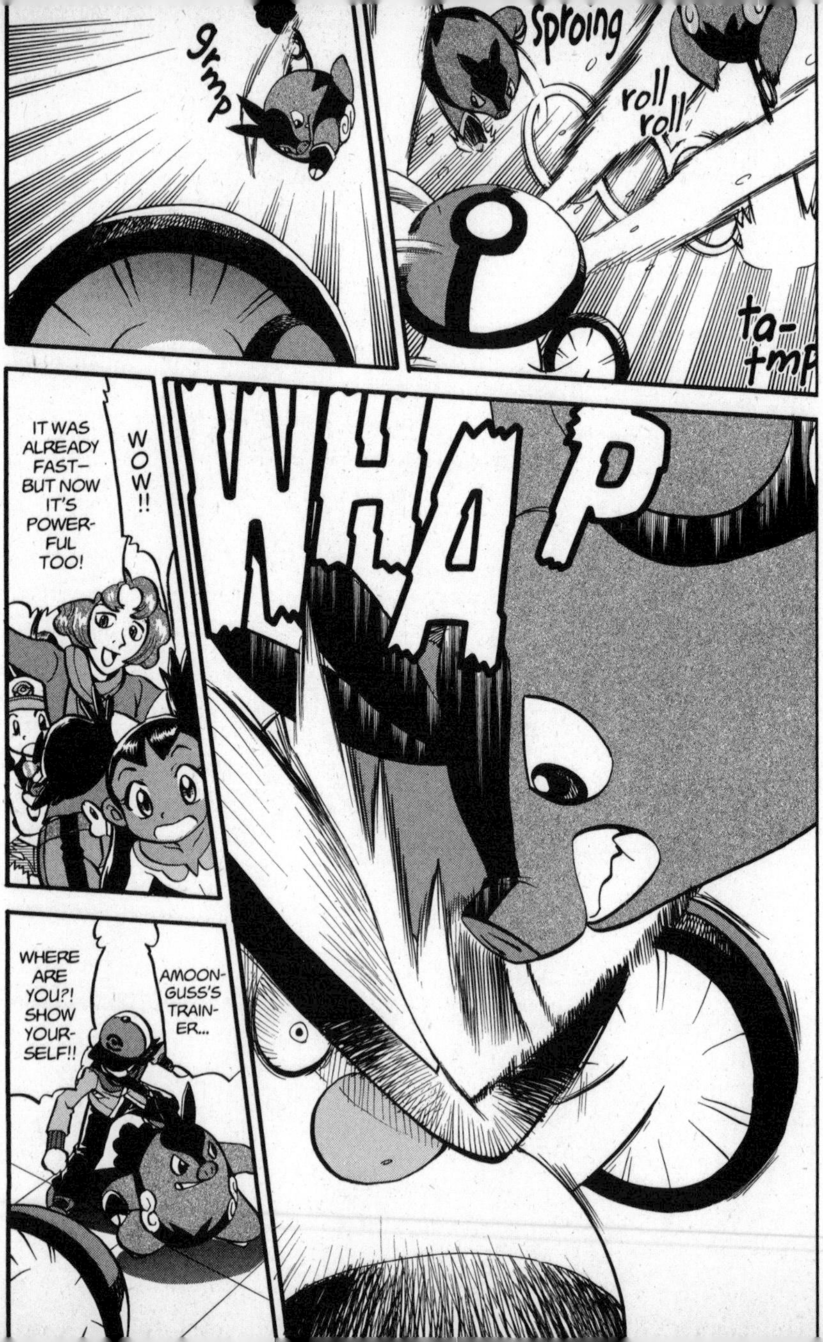
sproing
roll roll
ta-tmp
grmp
WHAP
WOW!!
IT WAS ALREADY FAST—BUT NOW IT'S POWERFUL TOO!
AMOONGUSS'S TRAINER...
WHERE ARE YOU?! SHOW YOURSELF!!

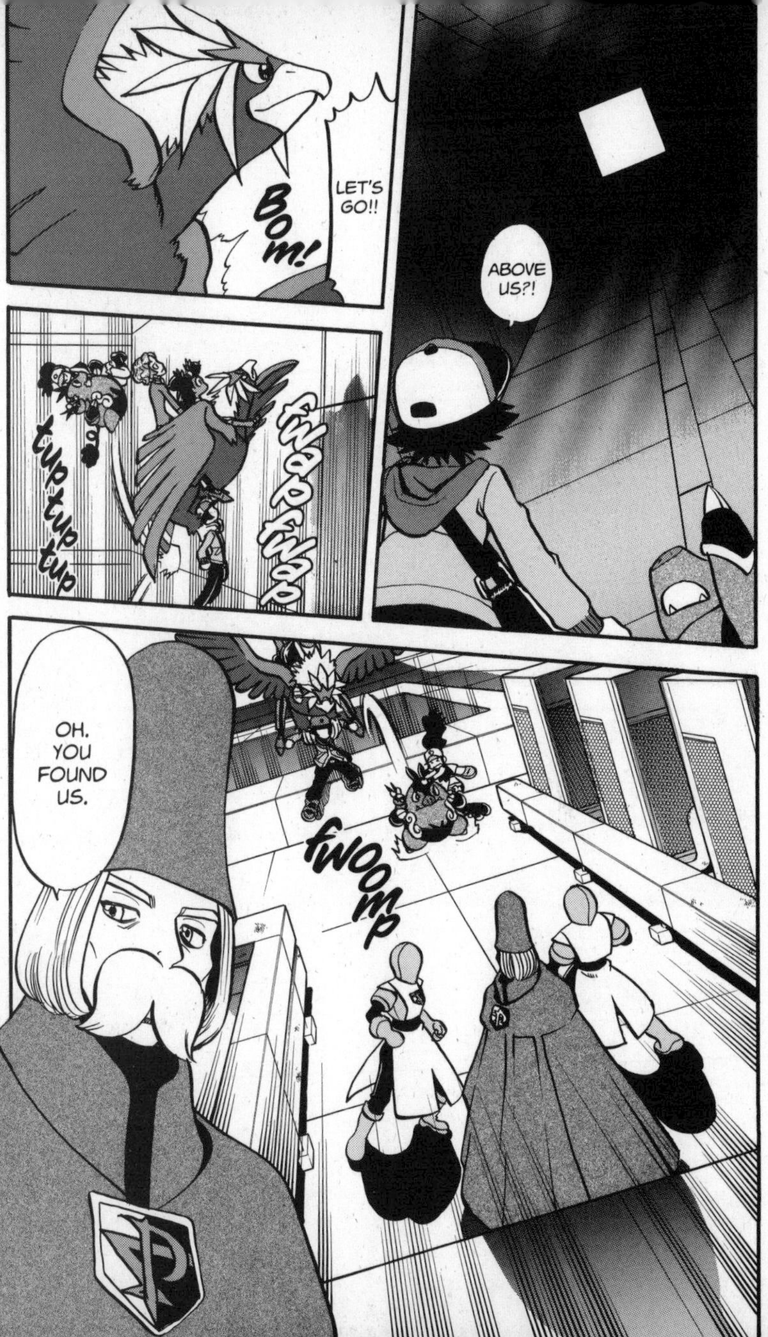
ABOVE US?!
LET'S GO!!
BOOM!
FWAP FWAP
TUP TUP TUP
OH. YOU FOUND US.
FWOOMP

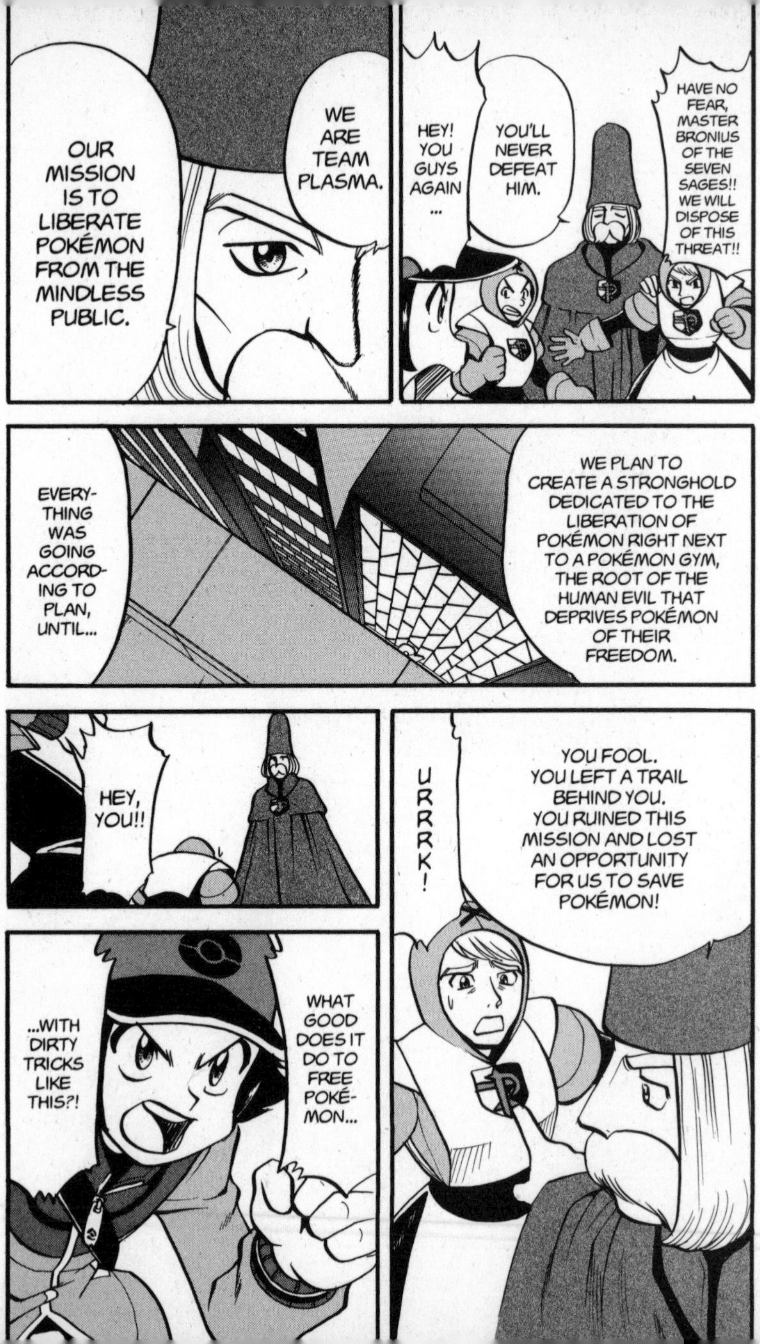
WE ARE TEAM PLASMA.
OUR MISSION IS TO LIBERATE POKéMON FROM THE MINDLESS PUBLIC.
HEY! YOU GUYS AGAIN ...
YOU'LL NEVER DEFEAT HIM.
HAVE NO FEAR, MASTER BRONIUS OF THE SEVEN SAGES!! WE WILL DISPOSE OF THIS THREAT!!
WE PLAN TO CREATE A STRONGHOLD DEDICATED TO THE LIBERATION OF POKéMON RIGHT NEXT TO A POKéMON GYM, THE ROOT OF THE HUMAN EVIL THAT DEPRIVES POKéMON OF THEIR FREEDOM.
EVERY-THING WAS GOING ACCORD-ING TO PLAN, UNTIL...
HEY, YOU!!
YOU FOOL. YOU LEFT A TRAIL BEHIND YOU. YOU RUINED THIS MISSION AND LOST AN OPPORTUNITY FOR US TO SAVE POKéMON!
URRRK!
WHAT GOOD DOES IT DO TO FREE POKé-MON...
...WITH DIRTY TRICKS LIKE THIS?!

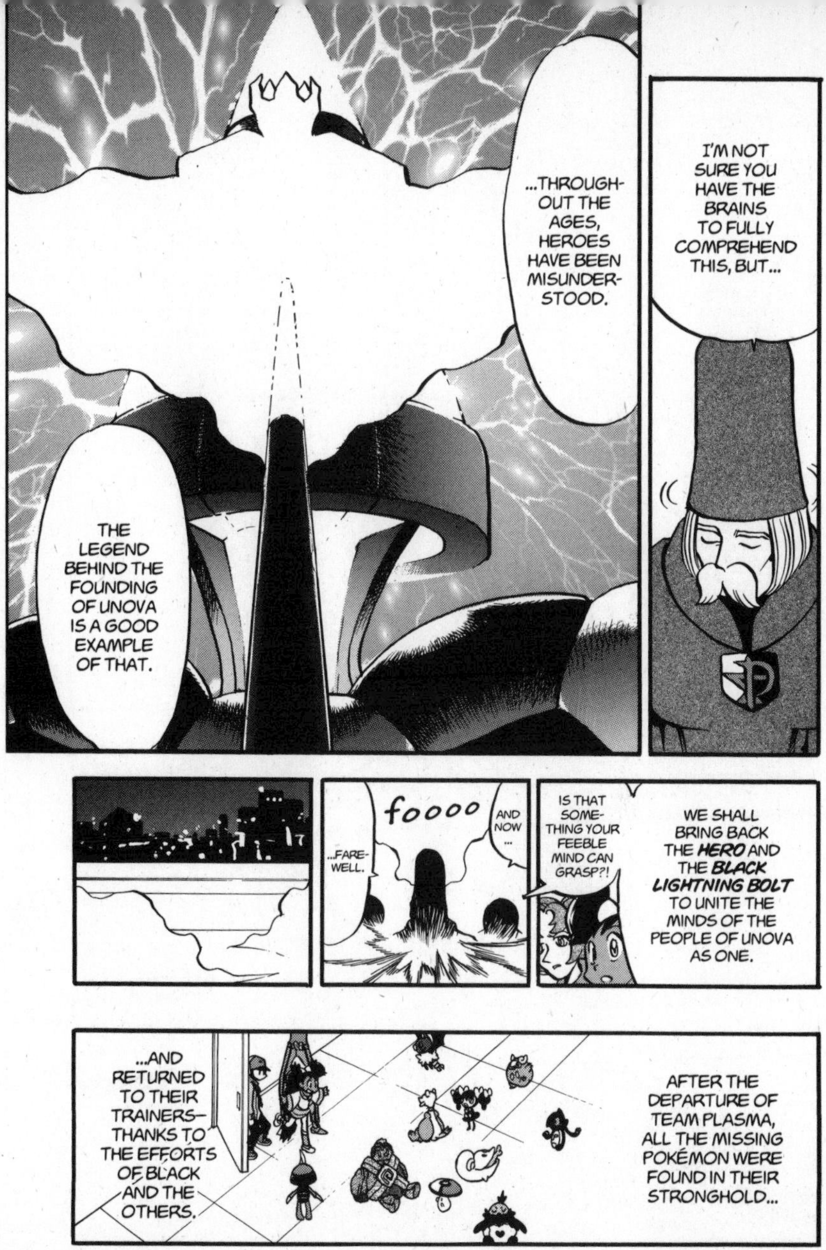
I'M NOT SURE YOU HAVE THE BRAINS TO FULLY COMPREHEND THIS, BUT...
...THROUGH-OUT THE AGES, HEROES HAVE BEEN MISUNDER-STOOD.
THE LEGEND BEHIND THE FOUNDING OF UNOVA IS A GOOD EXAMPLE OF THAT.
WE SHALL BRING BACK THE ***HERO*** AND THE ***BLACK LIGHTNING BOLT*** TO UNITE THE MINDS OF THE PEOPLE OF UNOVA AS ONE.
IS THAT SOME-THING YOUR FEEBLE MIND CAN GRASP?!
AND NOW ...
...FARE-WELL.
foooo
AFTER THE DEPARTURE OF TEAM PLASMA, ALL THE MISSING POKÉMON WERE FOUND IN THEIR STRONGHOLD...
...AND RETURNED TO THEIR TRAINERS— THANKS TO THE EFFORTS OF BLACK AND THE OTHERS.

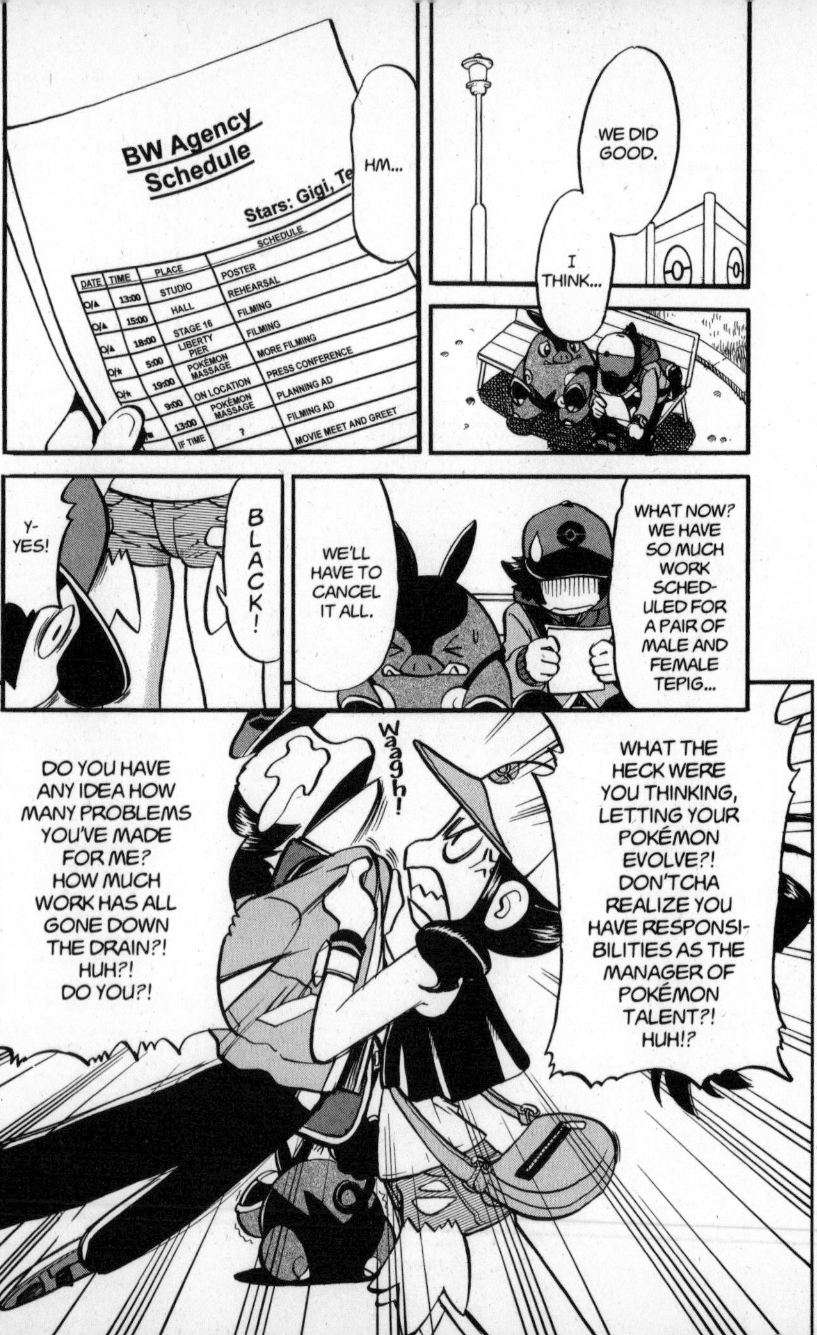
WE DID GOOD.
I THINK...
BW Agency Schedule
Stars: Gigi, Te
DATE TIME PLACE SCHEDULE
13:00 STUDIO POSTER
15:00 HALL REHEARSAL
18:00 STAGE 16 FILMING
5:00 LIBERTY PIER FILMING
19:00 POKÉMON MASSAGE MORE FILMING
9:00 ON LOCATION PRESS CONFERENCE
13:00 POKÉMON MASSAGE PLANNING AD
IF TIME ? FILMING AD
MOVIE MEET AND GREET
HM...
WHAT NOW? WE HAVE SO MUCH WORK SCHED-ULED FOR A PAIR OF MALE AND FEMALE TEPIG...
WE'LL HAVE TO CANCEL IT ALL.
BLACK!
Y-YES!
Waagh!
WHAT THE HECK WERE YOU THINKING, LETTING YOUR POKÉMON EVOLVE?! DON'TCHA REALIZE YOU HAVE RESPONSI-BILITIES AS THE MANAGER OF POKÉMON TALENT?! HUH!?
DO YOU HAVE ANY IDEA HOW MANY PROBLEMS YOU'VE MADE FOR ME? HOW MUCH WORK HAS ALL GONE DOWN THE DRAIN?! HUH?! DO YOU?!

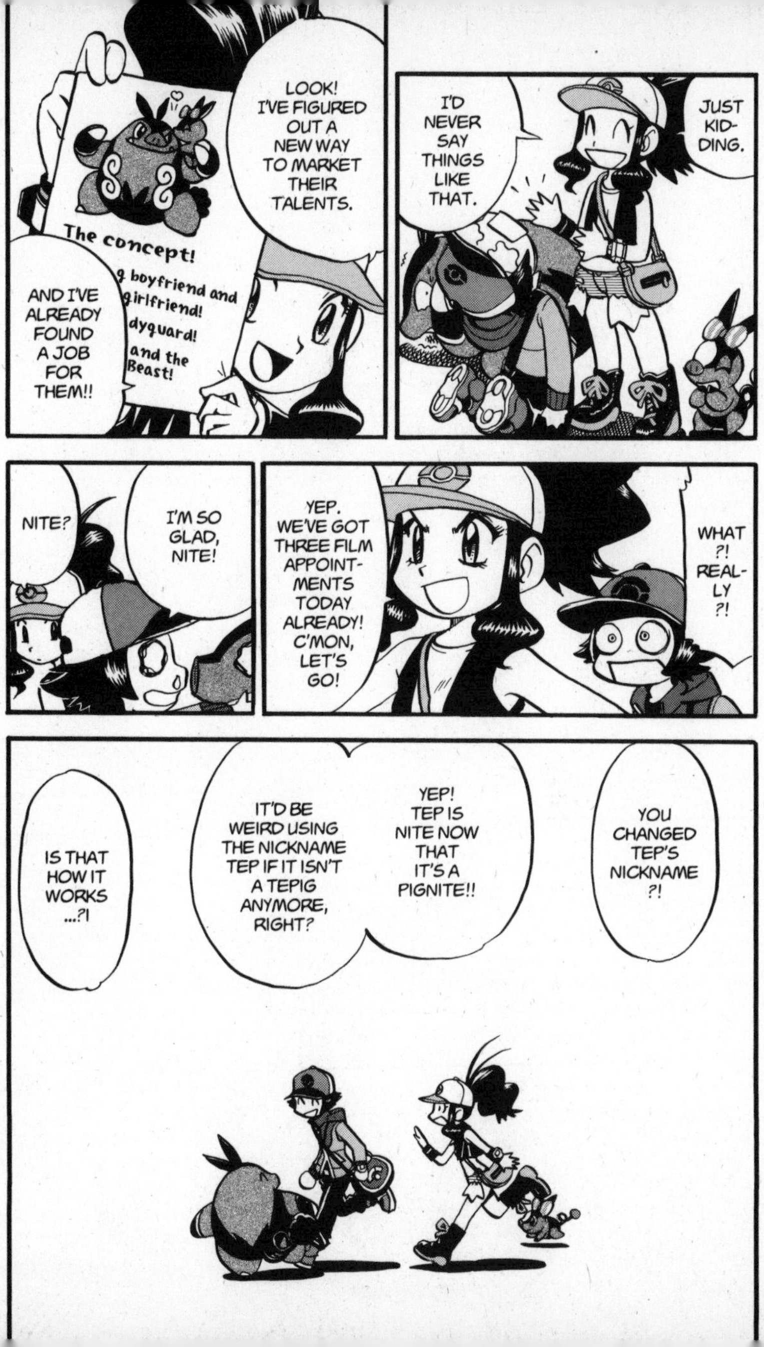
LOOK! I'VE FIGURED OUT A NEW WAY TO MARKET THEIR TALENTS.
The concept!
g boyfriend and girlfriend!
dyguard!
and the Beast!
AND I'VE ALREADY FOUND A JOB FOR THEM!!
I'D NEVER SAY THINGS LIKE THAT.
JUST KID-DING.
YEP. WE'VE GOT THREE FILM APPOINT-MENTS TODAY ALREADY! C'MON, LET'S GO!
WHAT?! REALLY?!
I'M SO GLAD, NITE!
NITE?
YOU CHANGED TEP'S NICKNAME?!
YEP! TEP IS NITE NOW THAT IT'S A PIGNITE!!
IT'D BE WEIRD USING THE NICKNAME TEP IF IT ISN'T A TEPIG ANYMORE, RIGHT?
IS THAT HOW IT WORKS...?!

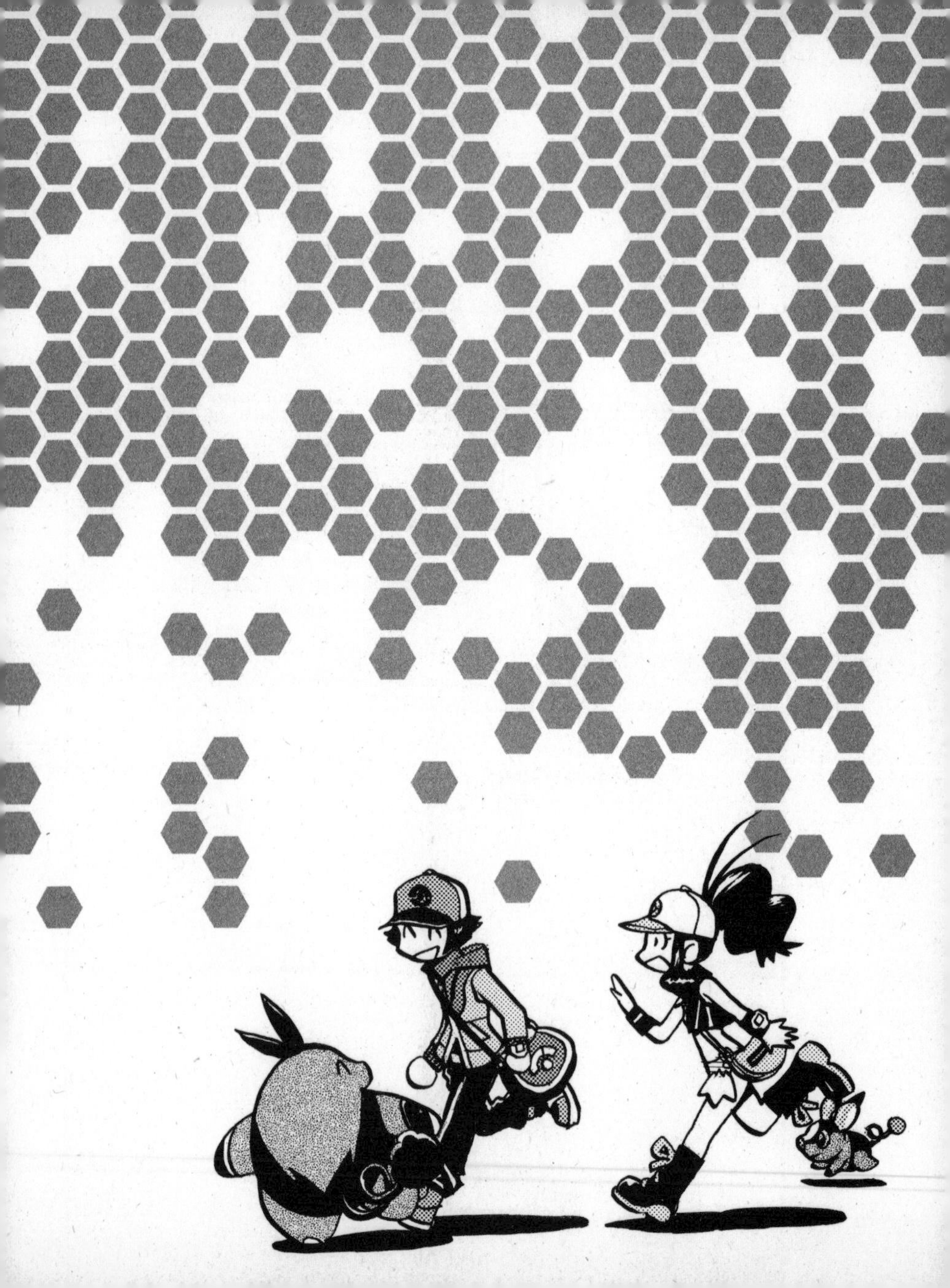

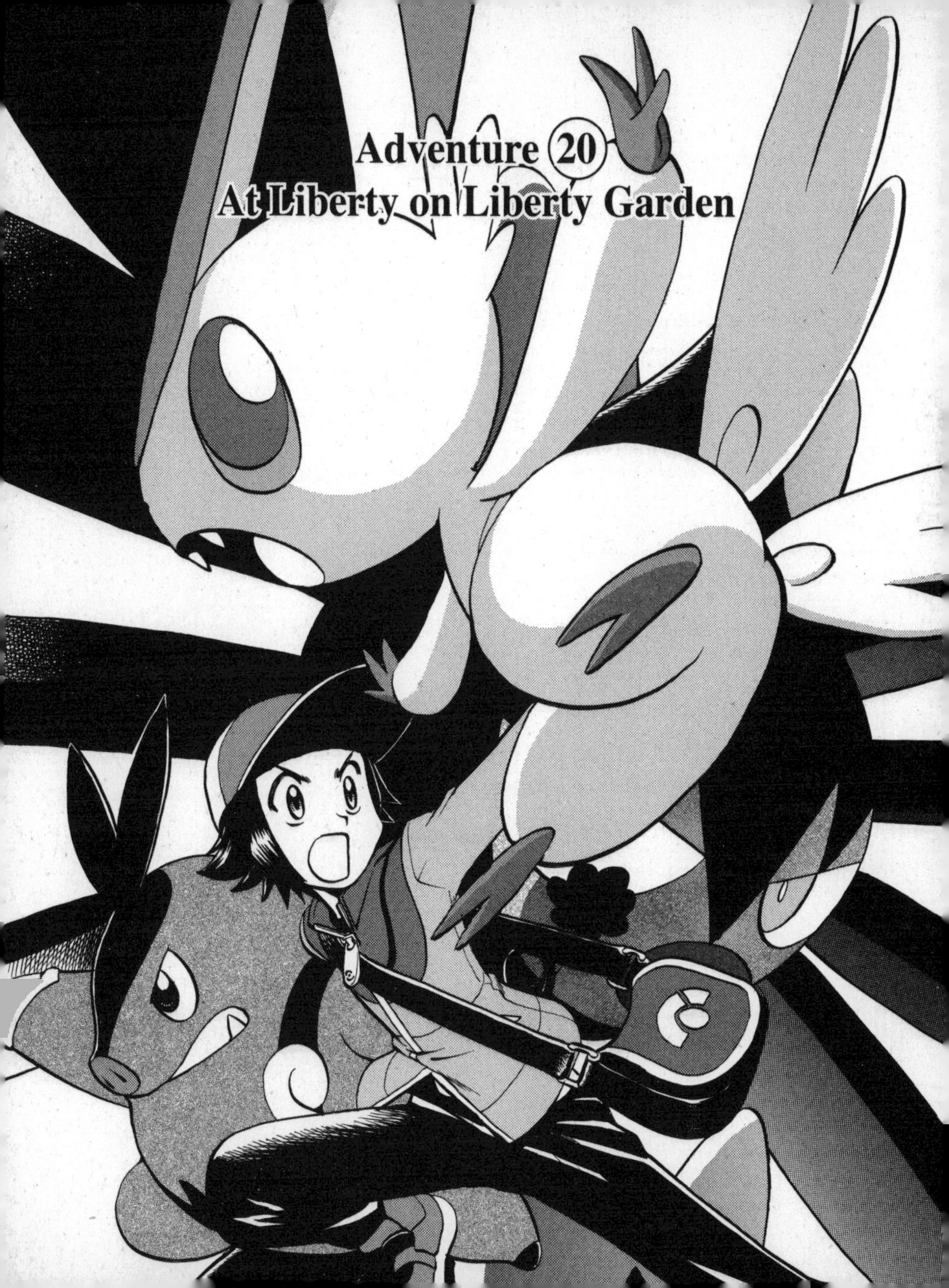
Adventure 20
At Liberty on Liberty Garden

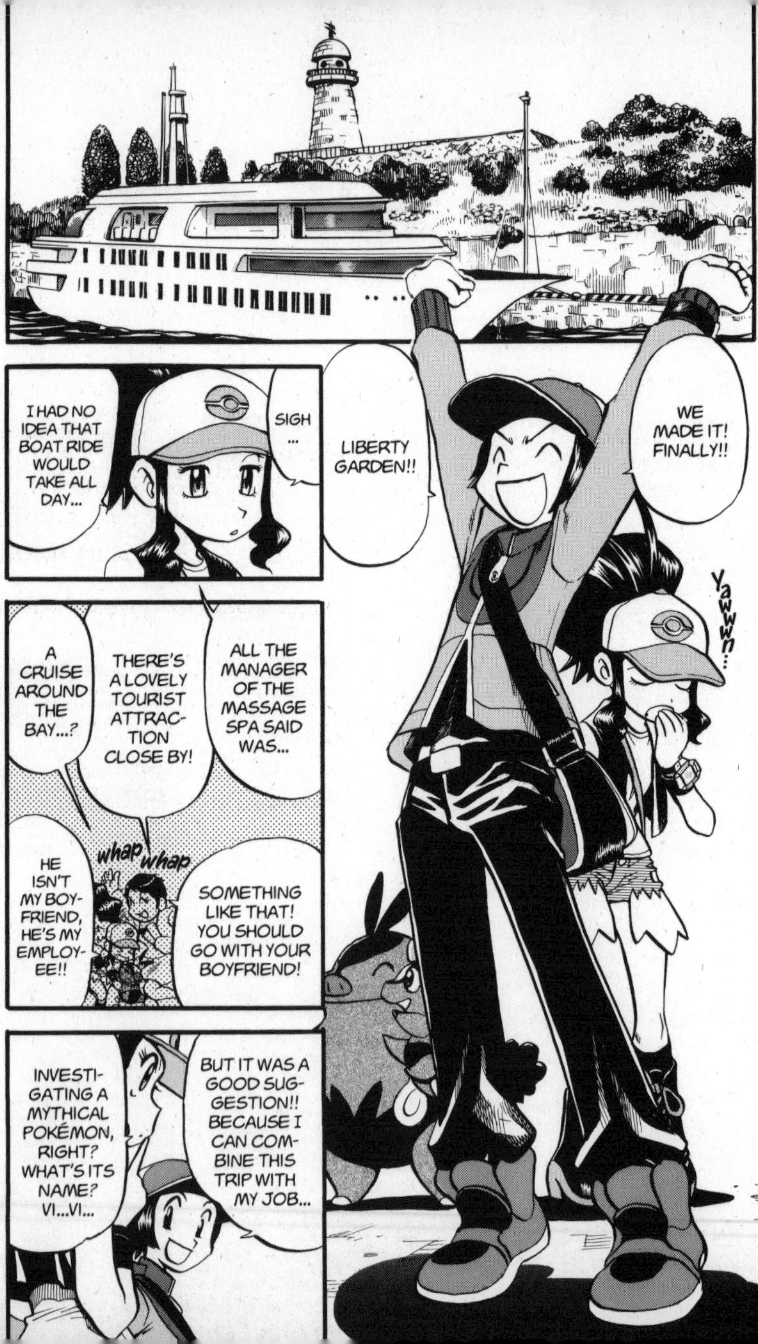

WE MADE IT! FINALLY!!
LIBERTY GARDEN!!
SIGH ...
I HAD NO IDEA THAT BOAT RIDE WOULD TAKE ALL DAY...
Yawwwn...
ALL THE MANAGER OF THE MASSAGE SPA SAID WAS...
THERE'S A LOVELY TOURIST ATTRACTION CLOSE BY!
A CRUISE AROUND THE BAY...?
SOMETHING LIKE THAT! YOU SHOULD GO WITH YOUR BOYFRIEND!
whap whap
HE ISN'T MY BOY-FRIEND, HE'S MY EMPLOY-EE!!
BUT IT WAS A GOOD SUG-GESTION!! BECAUSE I CAN COM-BINE THIS TRIP WITH MY JOB...
INVESTI-GATING A MYTHICAL POKÉMON, RIGHT? WHAT'S ITS NAME? VI...VI...

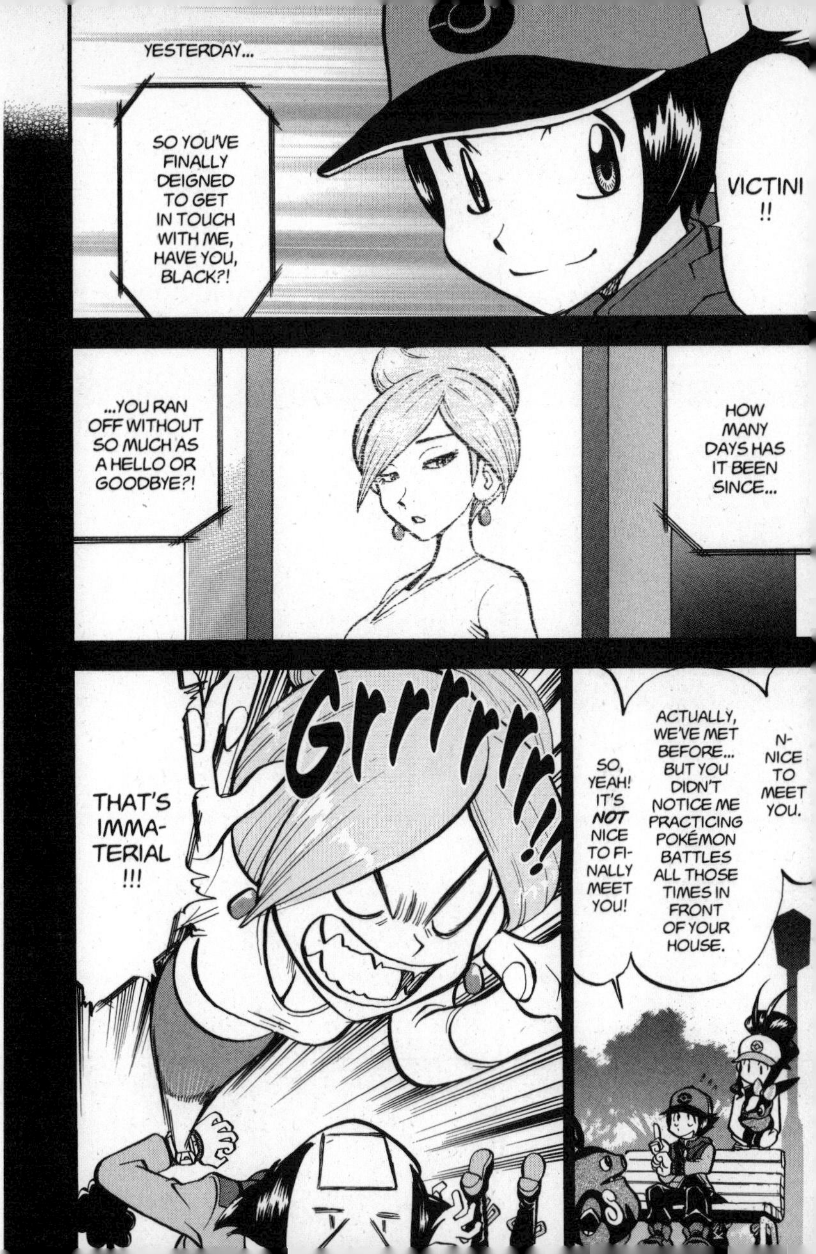

YESTERDAY...
VICTINI !!
SO YOU'VE FINALLY DEIGNED TO GET IN TOUCH WITH ME, HAVE YOU, BLACK?!
HOW MANY DAYS HAS IT BEEN SINCE...
...YOU RAN OFF WITHOUT SO MUCH AS A HELLO OR GOODBYE?!
N-NICE TO MEET YOU.
ACTUALLY, WE'VE MET BEFORE... BUT YOU DIDN'T NOTICE ME PRACTICING POKÉMON BATTLES ALL THOSE TIMES IN FRONT OF YOUR HOUSE.
SO, YEAH! IT'S NOT NICE TO FINALLY MEET YOU!
Grrrrrr!!
THAT'S IMMATERIAL!!!

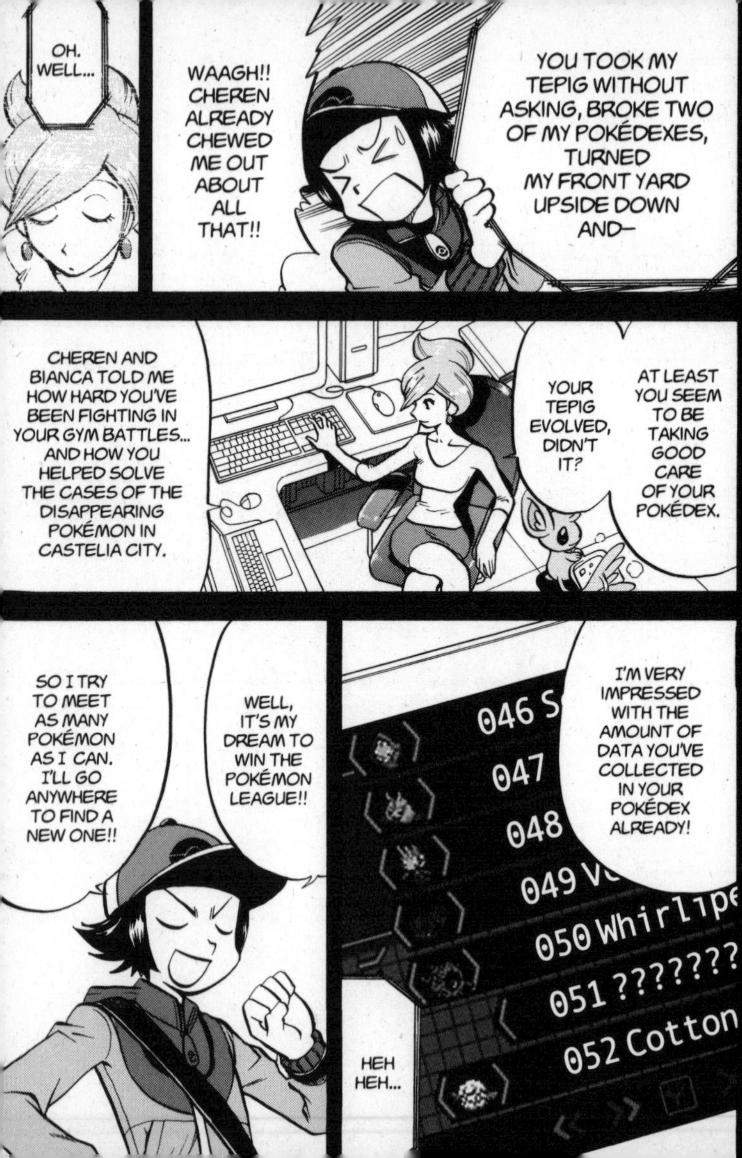
YOU TOOK MY TEPIG WITHOUT ASKING, BROKE TWO OF MY POKÉDEXES, TURNED MY FRONT YARD UPSIDE DOWN AND—
WAAGH!! CHEREN ALREADY CHEWED ME OUT ABOUT ALL THAT!!
OH. WELL...
AT LEAST YOU SEEM TO BE TAKING GOOD CARE OF YOUR POKÉDEX.
YOUR TEPIG EVOLVED, DIDN'T IT?
CHEREN AND BIANCA TOLD ME HOW HARD YOU'VE BEEN FIGHTING IN YOUR GYM BATTLES... AND HOW YOU HELPED SOLVE THE CASES OF THE DISAPPEARING POKÉMON IN CASTELIA CITY.
I'M VERY IMPRESSED WITH THE AMOUNT OF DATA YOU'VE COLLECTED IN YOUR POKÉDEX ALREADY!
046 S
047
048
049 V
050 Whirlipe
051 ???????
052 Cotton
HEH HEH...
WELL, IT'S MY DREAM TO WIN THE POKÉMON LEAGUE!!
SO I TRY TO MEET AS MANY POKÉMON AS I CAN. I'LL GO ANYWHERE TO FIND A NEW ONE!!

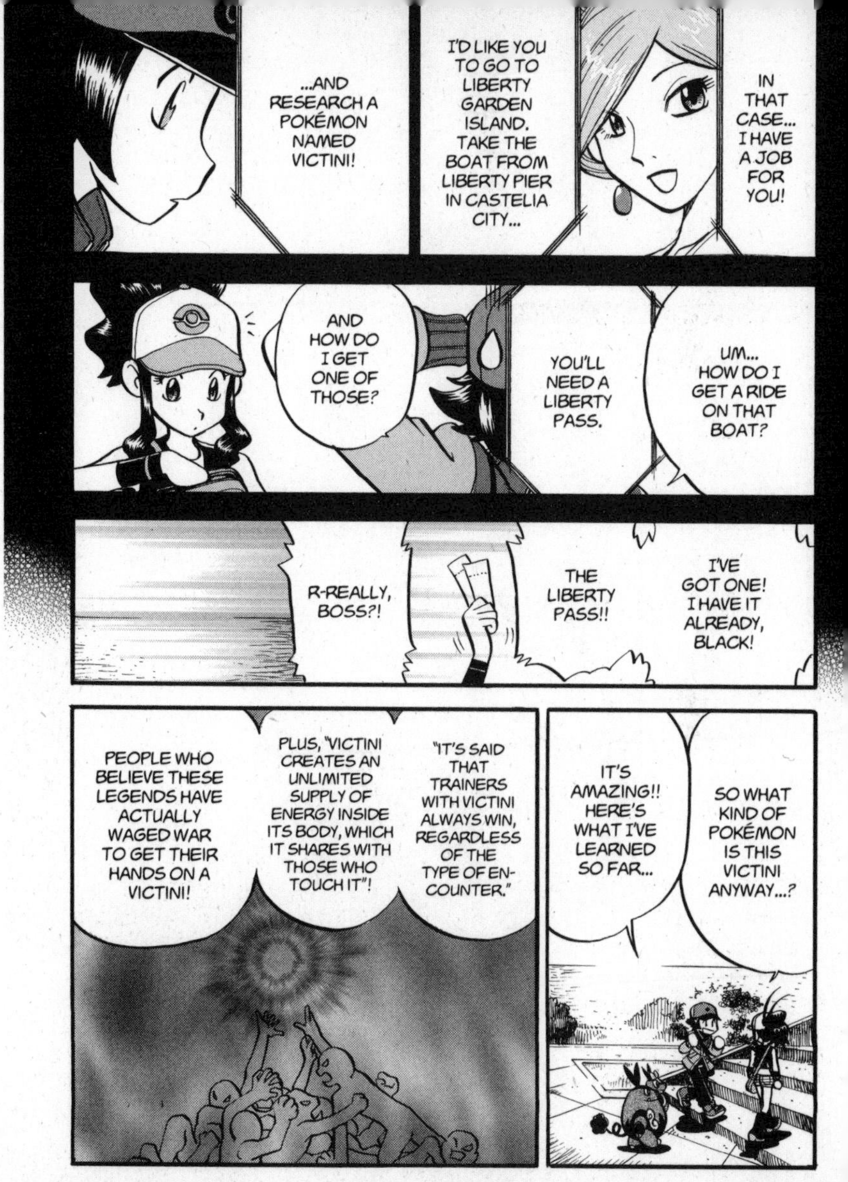
IN THAT CASE... I HAVE A JOB FOR YOU!
I'D LIKE YOU TO GO TO LIBERTY GARDEN ISLAND. TAKE THE BOAT FROM LIBERTY PIER IN CASTELIA CITY...
...AND RESEARCH A POKÉMON NAMED VICTINI!
UM... HOW DO I GET A RIDE ON THAT BOAT?
YOU'LL NEED A LIBERTY PASS.
AND HOW DO I GET ONE OF THOSE?
I'VE GOT ONE! I HAVE IT ALREADY, BLACK!
THE LIBERTY PASS!!
R-REALLY, BOSS?!
SO WHAT KIND OF POKÉMON IS THIS VICTINI ANYWAY...?
IT'S AMAZING!! HERE'S WHAT I'VE LEARNED SO FAR...
"IT'S SAID THAT TRAINERS WITH VICTINI ALWAYS WIN, REGARDLESS OF THE TYPE OF EN-COUNTER."
PLUS, "VICTINI CREATES AN UNLIMITED SUPPLY OF ENERGY INSIDE ITS BODY, WHICH IT SHARES WITH THOSE WHO TOUCH IT"!
PEOPLE WHO BELIEVE THESE LEGENDS HAVE ACTUALLY WAGED WAR TO GET THEIR HANDS ON A VICTINI!

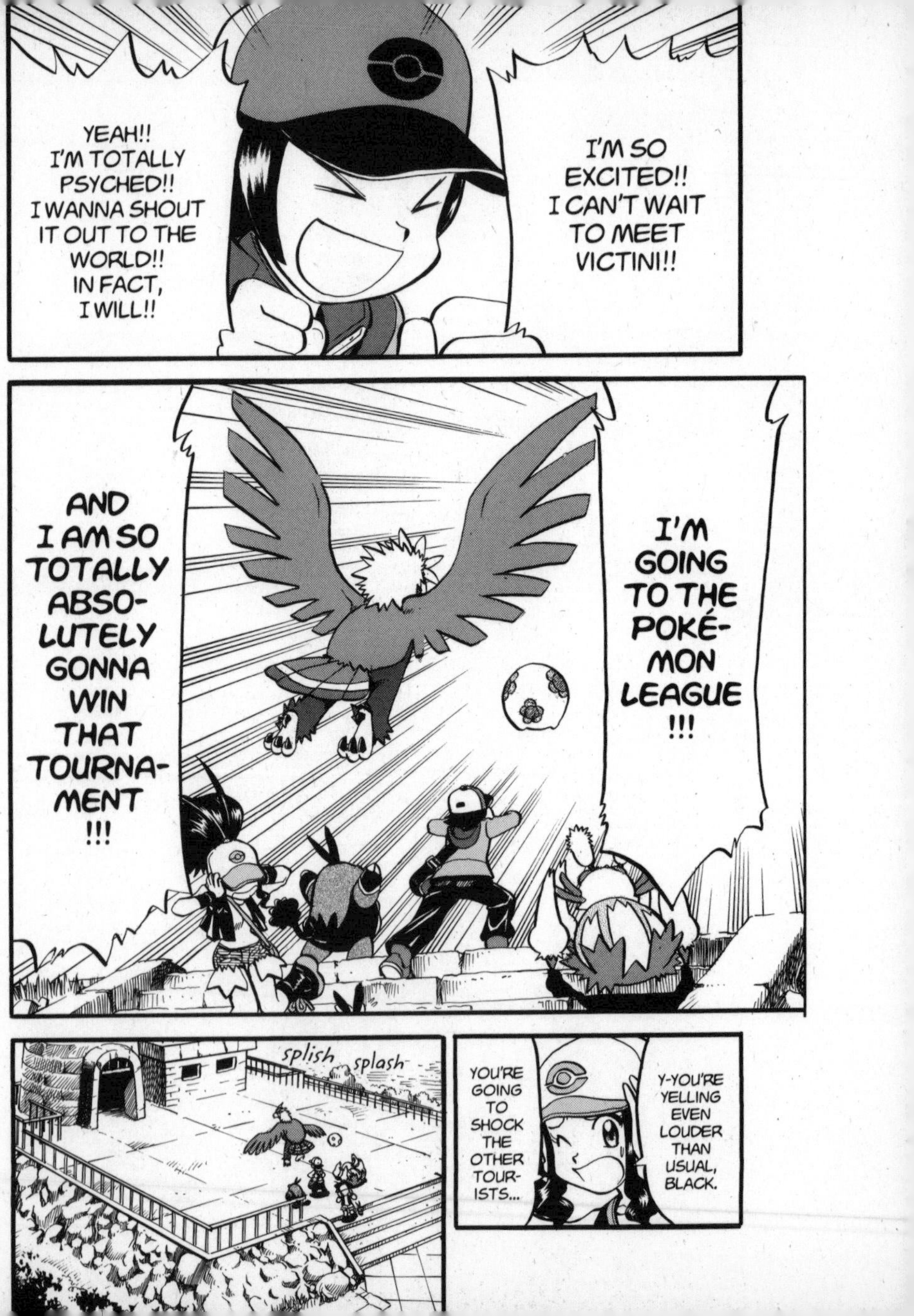
I'M SO EXCITED!! I CAN'T WAIT TO MEET VICTINI!!
YEAH!! I'M TOTALLY PSYCHED!! I WANNA SHOUT IT OUT TO THE WORLD!! IN FACT, I WILL!!
I'M GOING TO THE POKÉ-MON LEAGUE !!!
AND I AM SO TOTALLY ABSO-LUTELY GONNA WIN THAT TOURNA-MENT !!!
Y-YOU'RE YELLING EVEN LOUDER THAN USUAL, BLACK.
YOU'RE GOING TO SHOCK THE OTHER TOUR-ISTS...
splish
splash

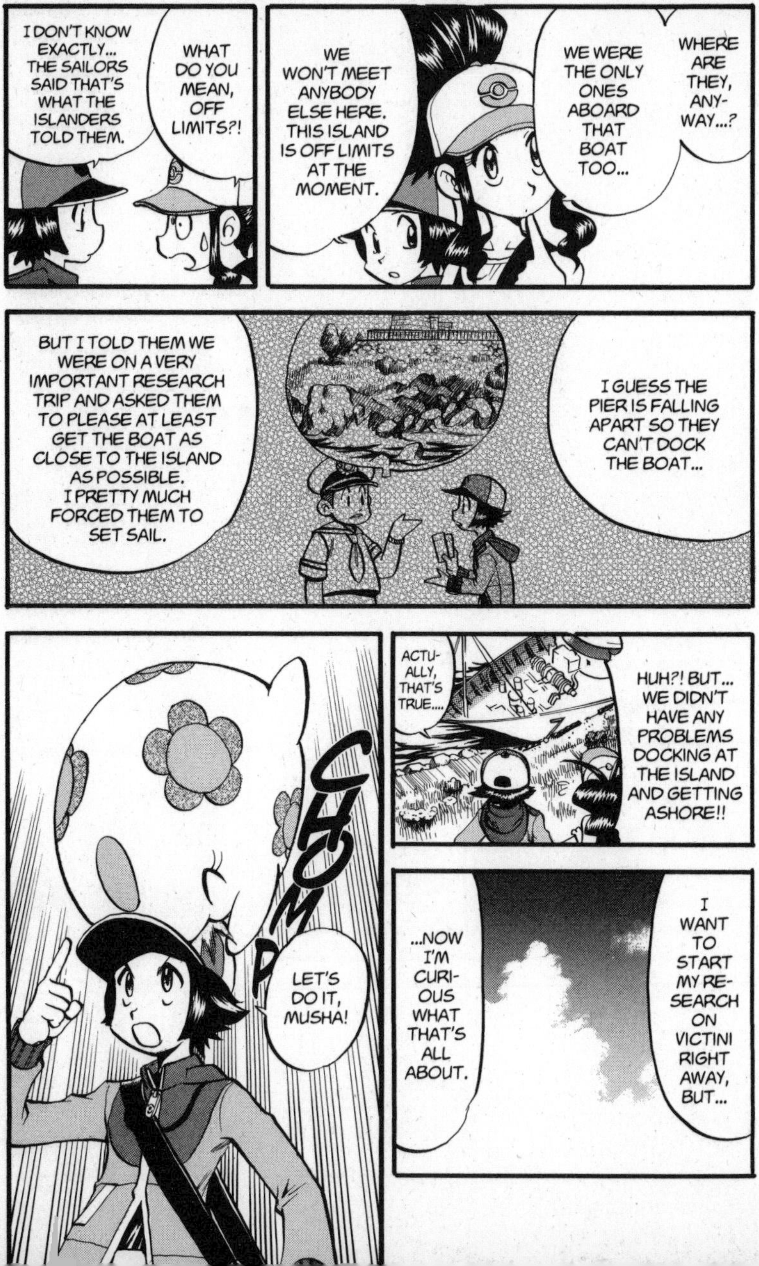

WHERE ARE THEY, ANY-WAY...?
WE WERE THE ONLY ONES ABOARD THAT BOAT TOO...
WE WON'T MEET ANYBODY ELSE HERE. THIS ISLAND IS OFF LIMITS AT THE MOMENT.
WHAT DO YOU MEAN, OFF LIMITS?!
I DON'T KNOW EXACTLY... THE SAILORS SAID THAT'S WHAT THE ISLANDERS TOLD THEM.
I GUESS THE PIER IS FALLING APART SO THEY CAN'T DOCK THE BOAT...
BUT I TOLD THEM WE WERE ON A VERY IMPORTANT RESEARCH TRIP AND ASKED THEM TO PLEASE AT LEAST GET THE BOAT AS CLOSE TO THE ISLAND AS POSSIBLE. I PRETTY MUCH FORCED THEM TO SET SAIL.
HUH?! BUT... WE DIDN'T HAVE ANY PROBLEMS DOCKING AT THE ISLAND AND GETTING ASHORE!!
ACTU-ALLY, THAT'S TRUE....
I WANT TO START MY RE-SEARCH ON VICTINI RIGHT AWAY, BUT...
...NOW I'M CURI-OUS WHAT THAT'S ALL ABOUT.
LET'S DO IT, MUSHA!
CHOMP

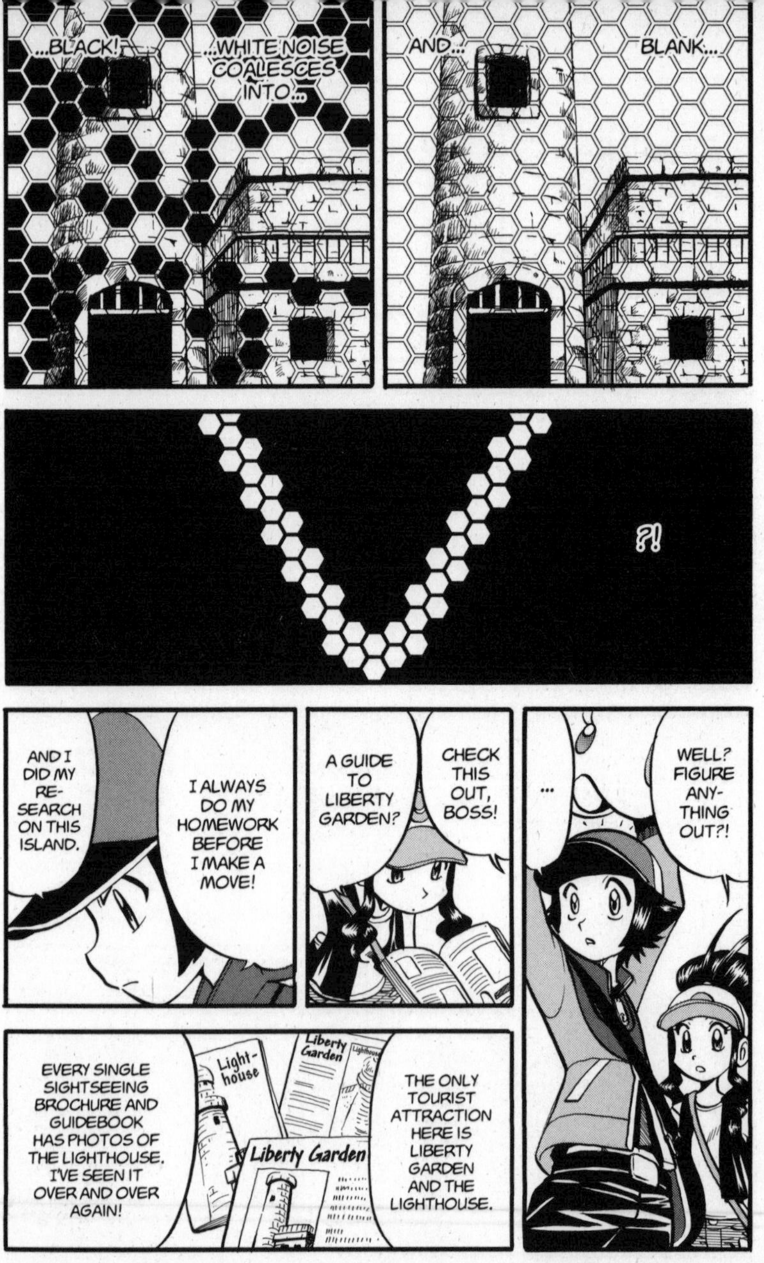
BLANK...
AND...
...WHITE NOISE COALESCES INTO...
...BLACK!
?!
WELL? FIGURE ANYTHING OUT?!
...
CHECK THIS OUT, BOSS!
A GUIDE TO LIBERTY GARDEN?
I ALWAYS DO MY HOMEWORK BEFORE I MAKE A MOVE!
AND I DID MY RESEARCH ON THIS ISLAND.
THE ONLY TOURIST ATTRACTION HERE IS LIBERTY GARDEN AND THE LIGHTHOUSE.
Light-house
Liberty Garden
Lighthouse
Liberty Garden
EVERY SINGLE SIGHTSEEING BROCHURE AND GUIDEBOOK HAS PHOTOS OF THE LIGHTHOUSE. I'VE SEEN IT OVER AND OVER AGAIN!

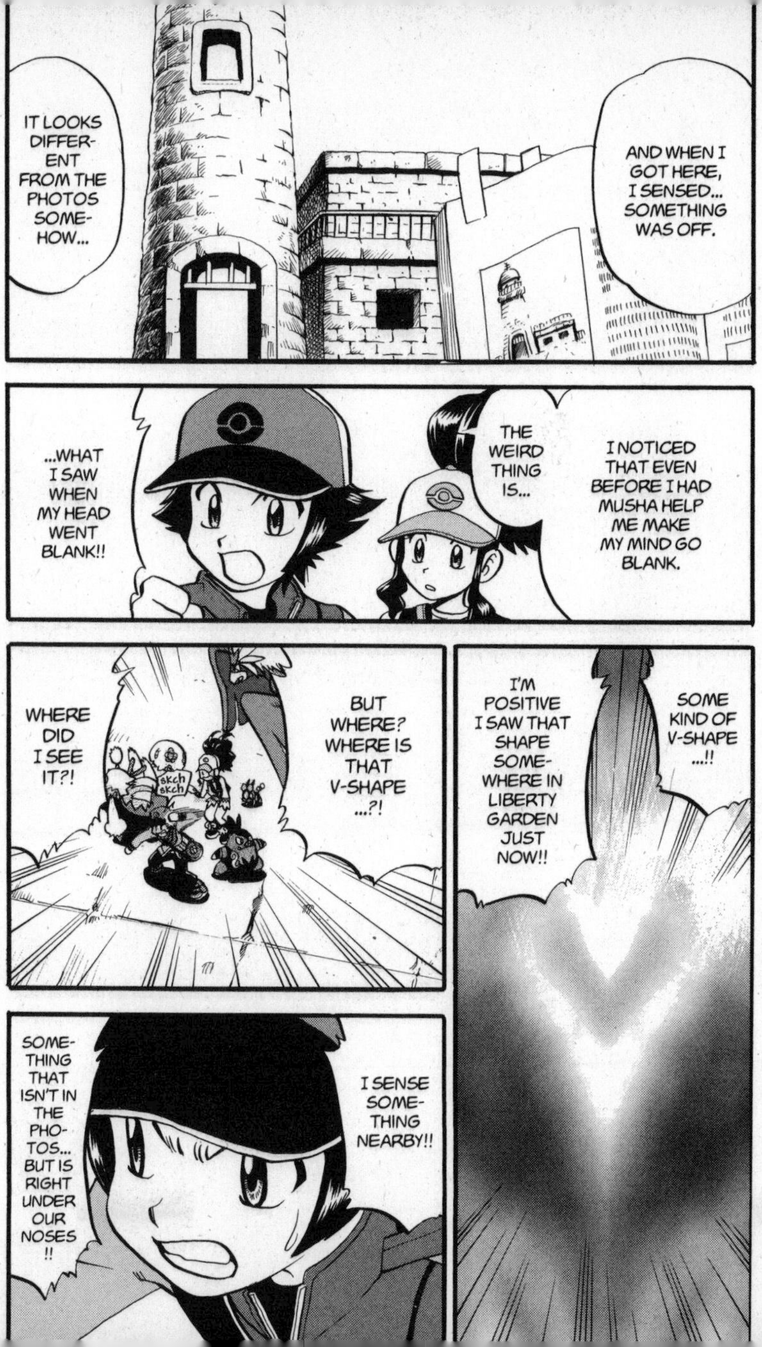
IT LOOKS DIFFERENT FROM THE PHOTOS SOMEHOW...
AND WHEN I GOT HERE, I SENSED... SOMETHING WAS OFF.
...WHAT I SAW WHEN MY HEAD WENT BLANK!!
THE WEIRD THING IS...
I NOTICED THAT EVEN BEFORE I HAD MUSHA HELP ME MAKE MY MIND GO BLANK.
WHERE DID I SEE IT?!
skch skch
BUT WHERE? WHERE IS THAT V-SHAPE ...?!
I'M POSITIVE I SAW THAT SHAPE SOMEWHERE IN LIBERTY GARDEN JUST NOW!!
SOME KIND OF V-SHAPE ...!!
SOMETHING THAT ISN'T IN THE PHOTOS... BUT IS RIGHT UNDER OUR NOSES !!
I SENSE SOMETHING NEARBY!!

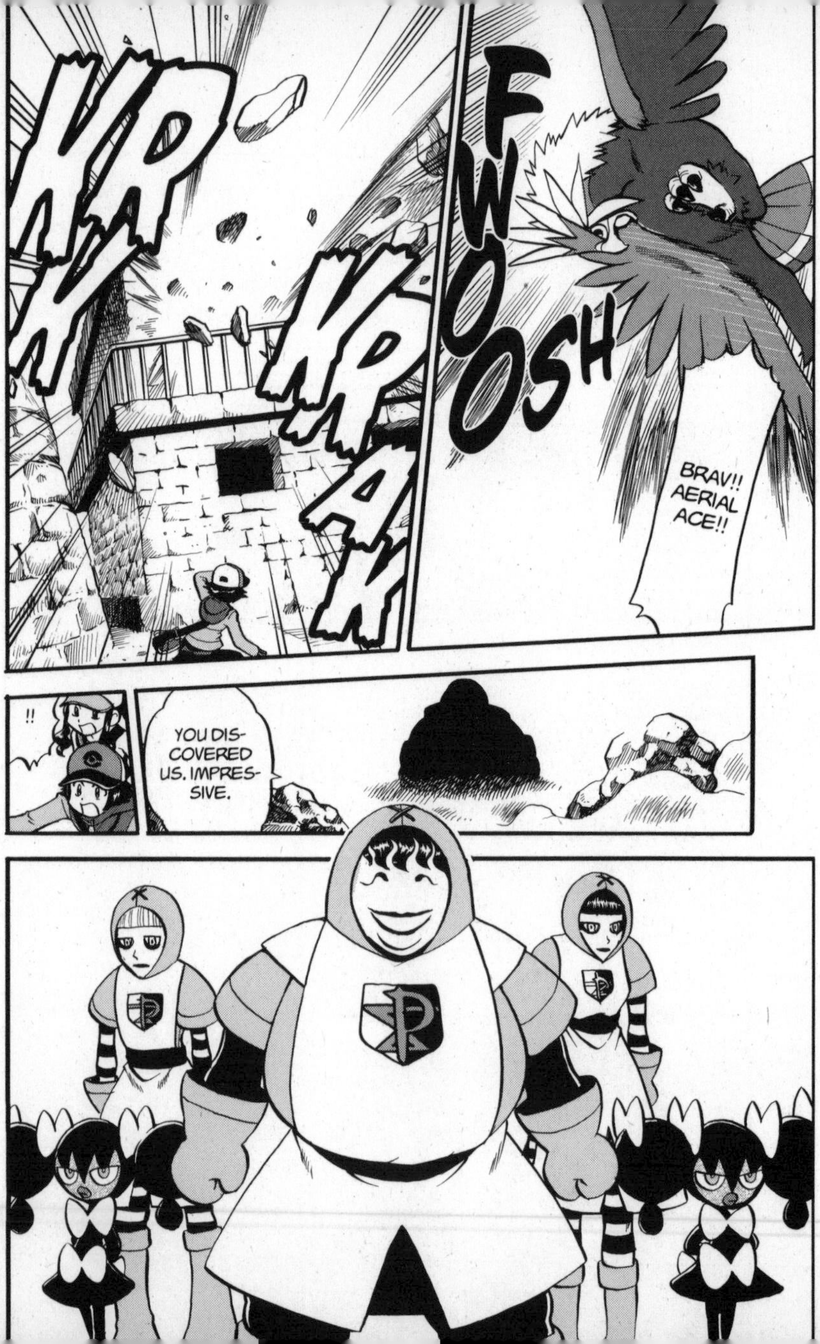
KRAK
FWOOOSH
BRAV!! AERIAL ACE!!
KRAK
!!
YOU DISCOVERED US. IMPRESSIVE.

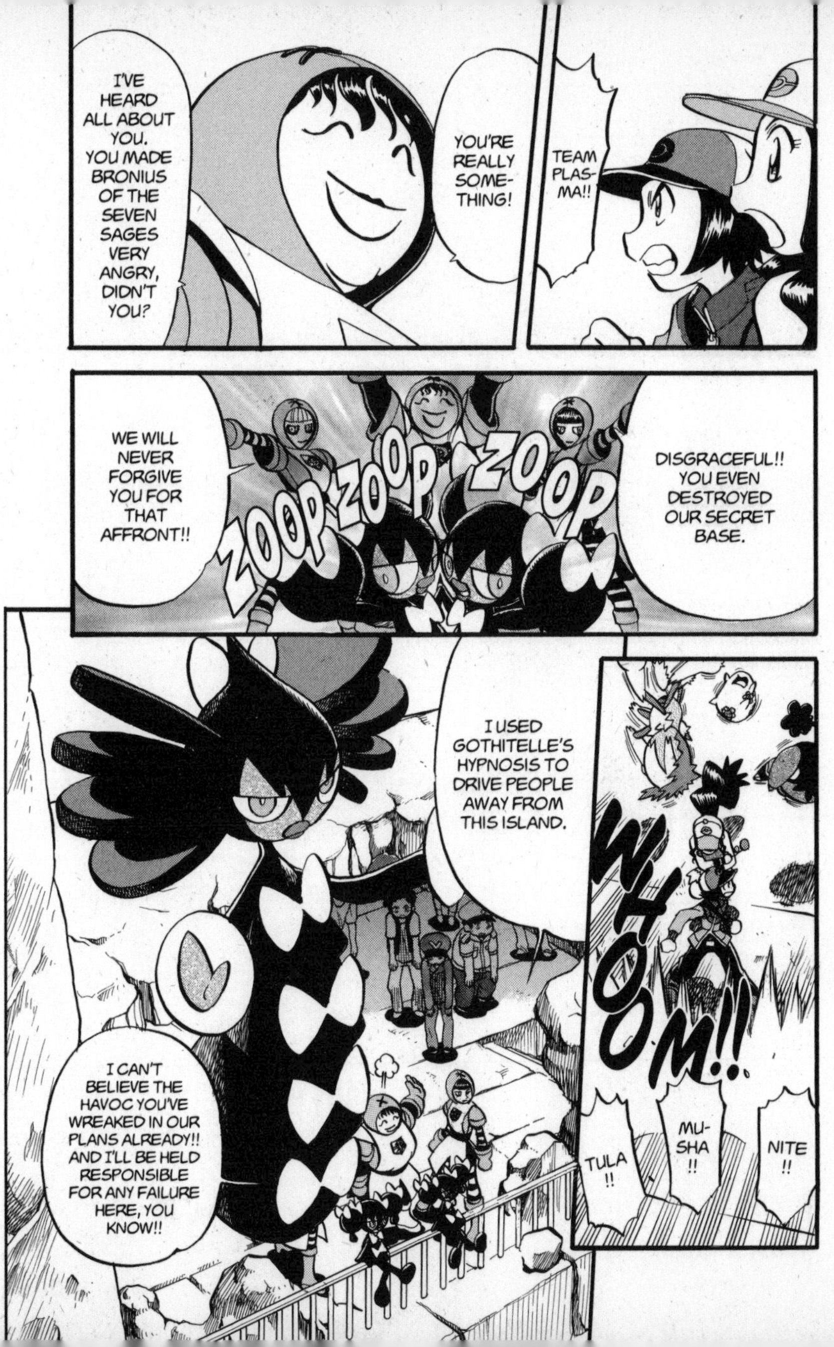
TEAM PLAS-MA!!
I'VE HEARD ALL ABOUT YOU. YOU MADE BRONIUS OF THE SEVEN SAGES VERY ANGRY, DIDN'T YOU?
YOU'RE REALLY SOME-THING!
DISGRACEFUL!! YOU EVEN DESTROYED OUR SECRET BASE.
ZOOP ZOOP ZOOP ZOOP
WE WILL NEVER FORGIVE YOU FOR THAT AFFRONT!!
WHOOOM!!
I USED GOTHITELLE'S HYPNOSIS TO DRIVE PEOPLE AWAY FROM THIS ISLAND.
NITE!!
MU-SHA!!
TULA!!
I CAN'T BELIEVE THE HAVOC YOU'VE WREAKED IN OUR PLANS ALREADY!! AND I'LL BE HELD RESPONSIBLE FOR ANY FAILURE HERE, YOU KNOW!!

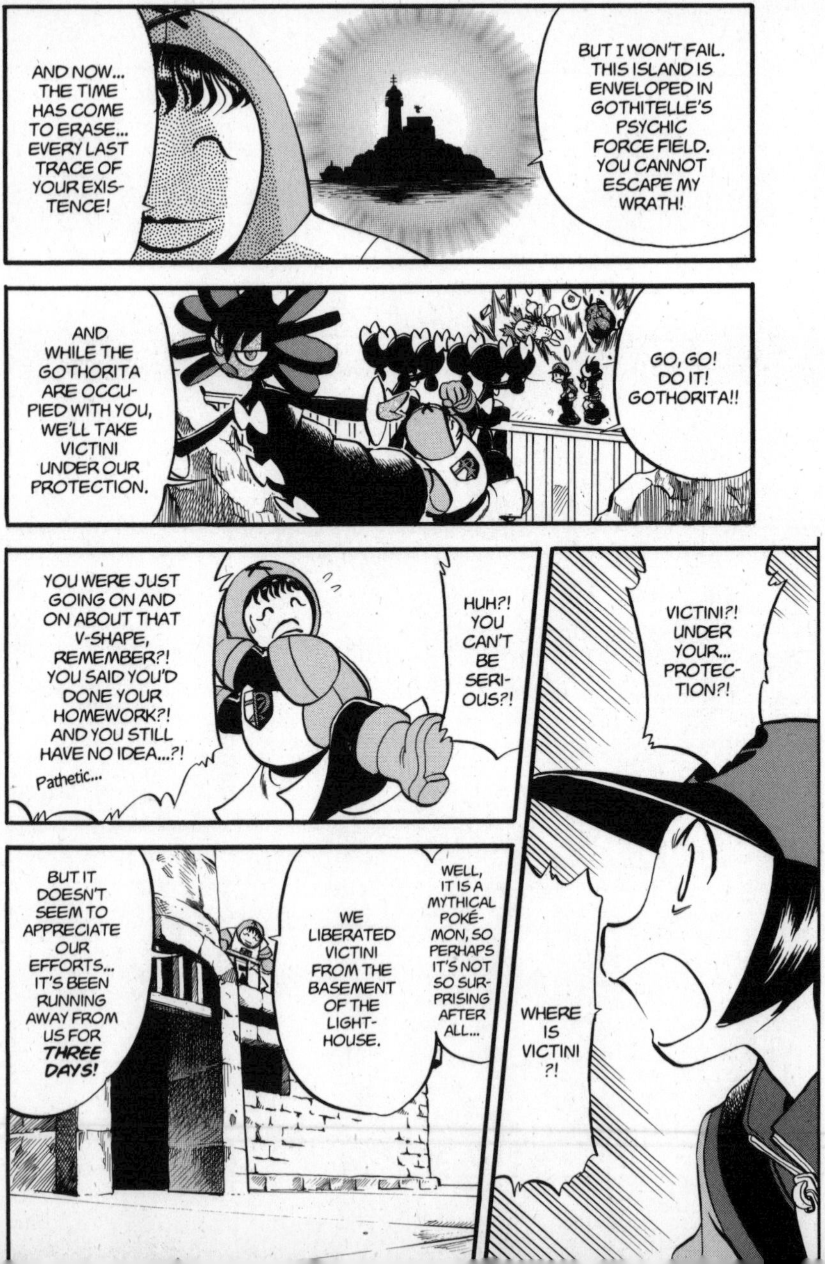
AND NOW... THE TIME HAS COME TO ERASE... EVERY LAST TRACE OF YOUR EXISTENCE!
BUT I WON'T FAIL. THIS ISLAND IS ENVELOPED IN GOTHITELLE'S PSYCHIC FORCE FIELD. YOU CANNOT ESCAPE MY WRATH!
AND WHILE THE GOTHORITA ARE OCCUPIED WITH YOU, WE'LL TAKE VICTINI UNDER OUR PROTECTION.
GO, GO! DO IT! GOTHORITA!!
YOU WERE JUST GOING ON AND ON ABOUT THAT V-SHAPE, REMEMBER?! YOU SAID YOU'D DONE YOUR HOMEWORK?! AND YOU STILL HAVE NO IDEA...?!
Pathetic...
HUH?! YOU CAN'T BE SERIOUS?!
VICTINI?! UNDER YOUR... PROTECTION?!
BUT IT DOESN'T SEEM TO APPRECIATE OUR EFFORTS... IT'S BEEN RUNNING AWAY FROM US FOR ***THREE DAYS!***
WE LIBERATED VICTINI FROM THE BASEMENT OF THE LIGHTHOUSE.
WELL, IT IS A MYTHICAL POKÉMON, SO PERHAPS IT'S NOT SO SURPRISING AFTER ALL...
WHERE IS VICTINI?!

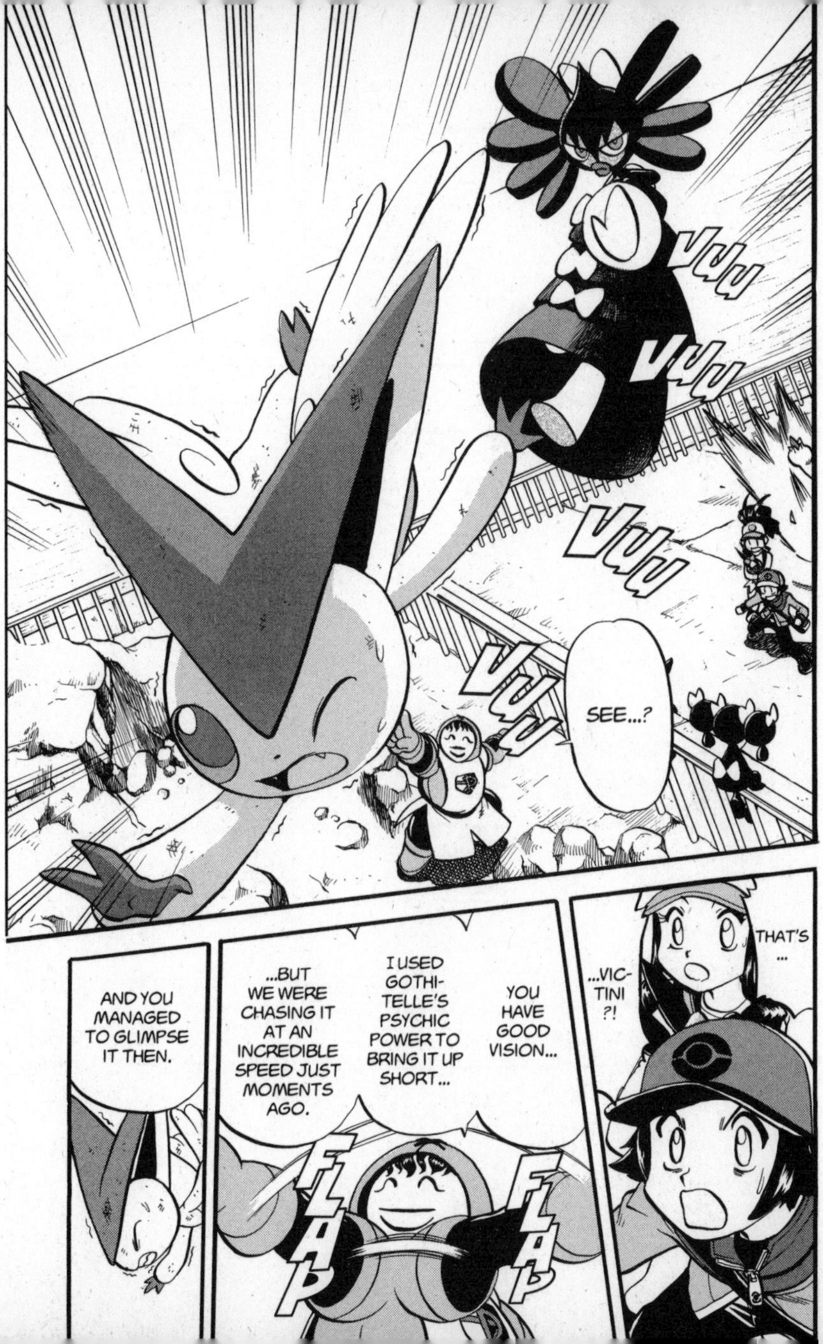
VUU
VUU
VUU
VUU
SEE...?
THAT'S ...
...VICTINI?!
YOU HAVE GOOD VISION...
I USED GOTHITELLE'S PSYCHIC POWER TO BRING IT UP SHORT...
...BUT WE WERE CHASING IT AT AN INCREDIBLE SPEED JUST MOMENTS AGO.
AND YOU MANAGED TO GLIMPSE IT THEN.
FLAP
FLAP

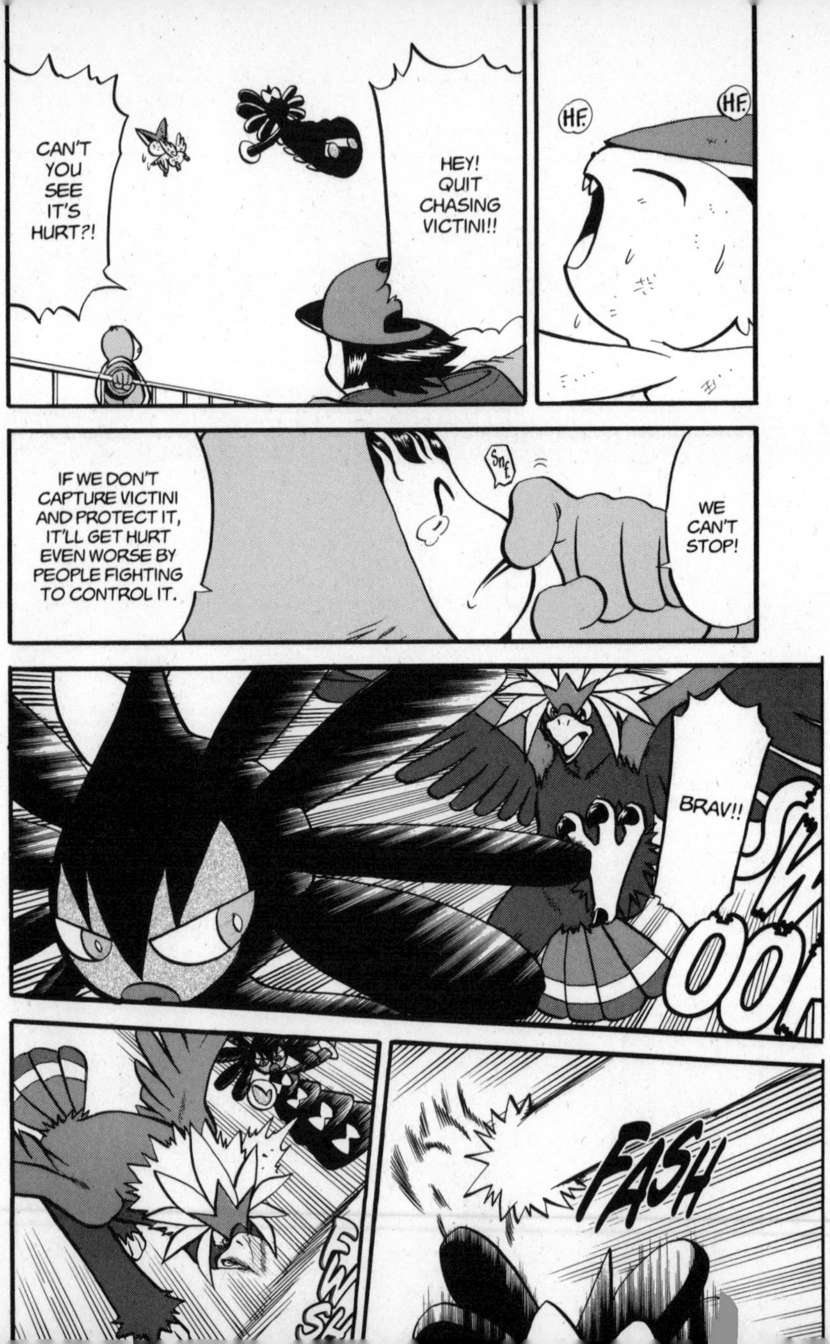
HF.
HF.
HEY! QUIT CHASING VICTINI!!
CAN'T YOU SEE IT'S HURT?!
WE CAN'T STOP!
Snf.
IF WE DON'T CAPTURE VICTINI AND PROTECT IT, IT'LL GET HURT EVEN WORSE BY PEOPLE FIGHTING TO CONTROL IT.
BRAV!!
SWOOO
FASH

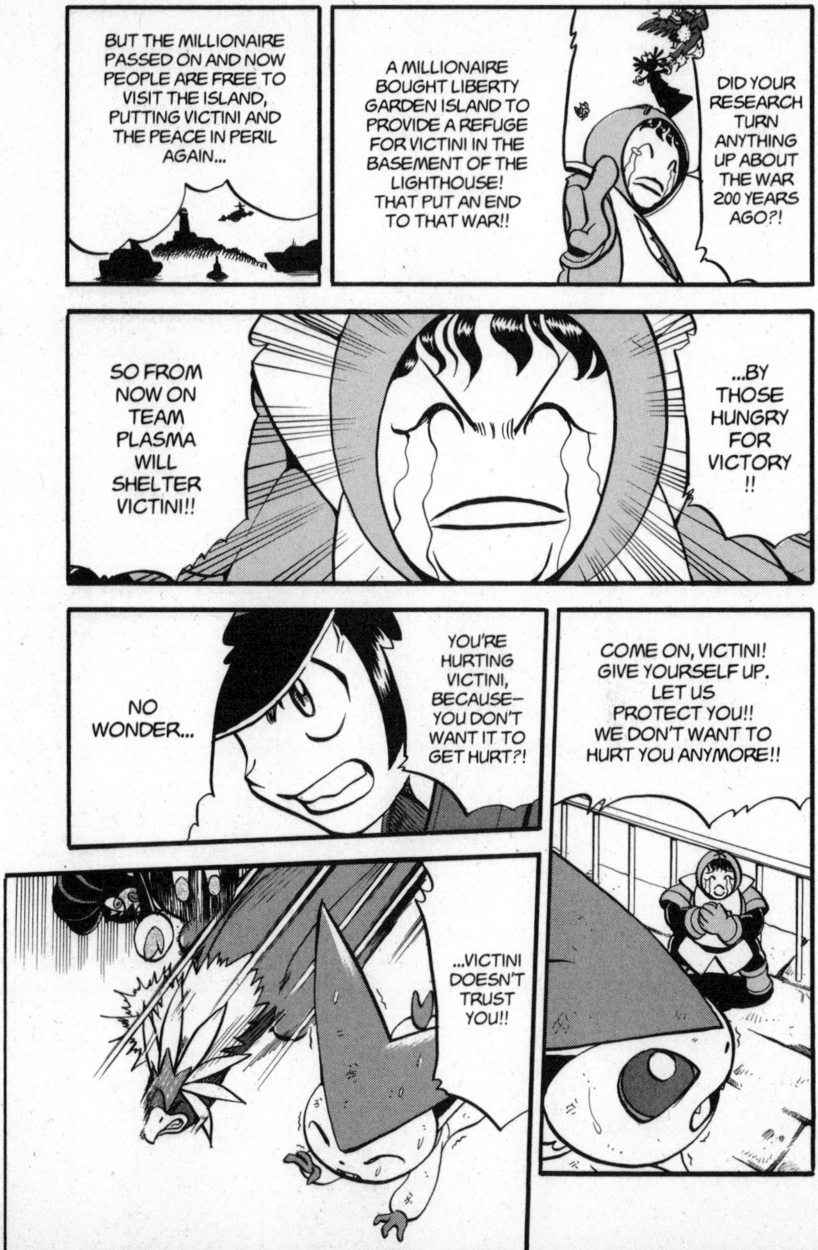
BUT THE MILLIONAIRE PASSED ON AND NOW PEOPLE ARE FREE TO VISIT THE ISLAND, PUTTING VICTINI AND THE PEACE IN PERIL AGAIN...
A MILLIONAIRE BOUGHT LIBERTY GARDEN ISLAND TO PROVIDE A REFUGE FOR VICTINI IN THE BASEMENT OF THE LIGHTHOUSE! THAT PUT AN END TO THAT WAR!!
DID YOUR RESEARCH TURN ANYTHING UP ABOUT THE WAR 200 YEARS AGO?!
SO FROM NOW ON TEAM PLASMA WILL SHELTER VICTINI!!
...BY THOSE HUNGRY FOR VICTORY!!
NO WONDER...
YOU'RE HURTING VICTINI, BECAUSE— YOU DON'T WANT IT TO GET HURT?!
COME ON, VICTINI! GIVE YOURSELF UP. LET US PROTECT YOU!! WE DON'T WANT TO HURT YOU ANYMORE!!
...VICTINI DOESN'T TRUST YOU!!

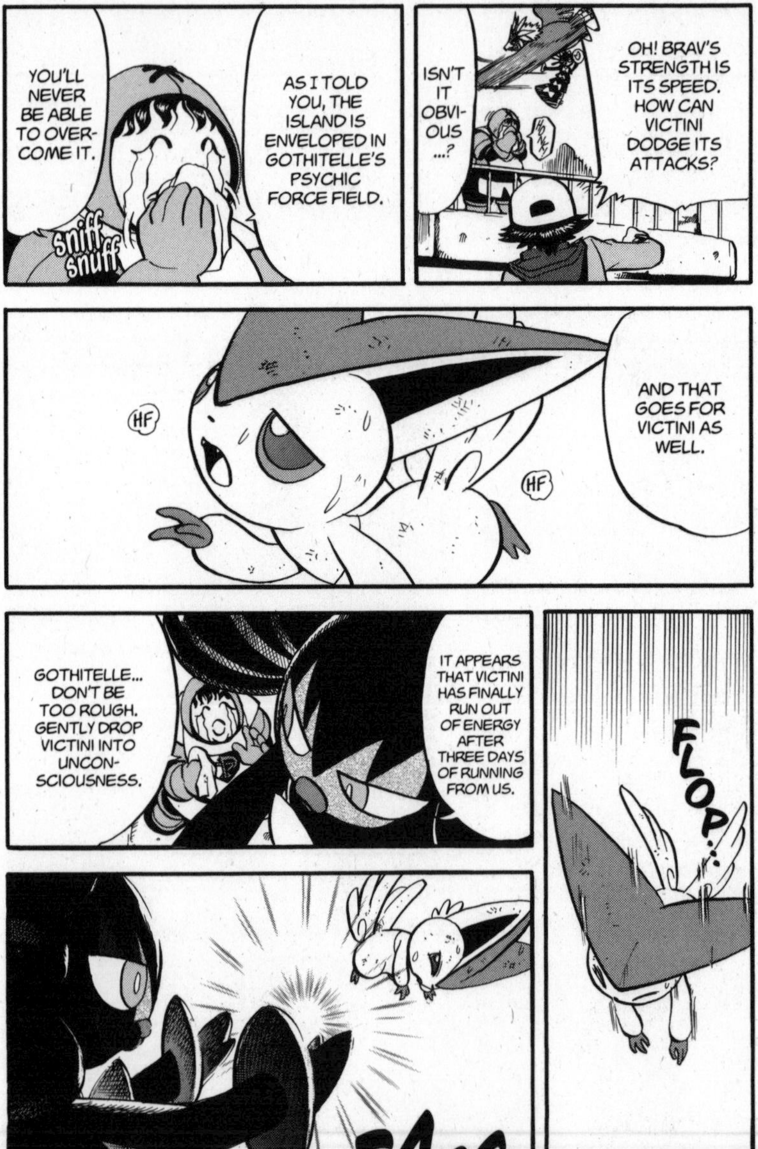
YOU'LL NEVER BE ABLE TO OVERCOME IT.
AS I TOLD YOU, THE ISLAND IS ENVELOPED IN GOTHITELLE'S PSYCHIC FORCE FIELD.
sniff snuff
ISN'T IT OBVIOUS ...?
OH! BRAV'S STRENGTH IS ITS SPEED. HOW CAN VICTINI DODGE ITS ATTACKS?
HF
HF
AND THAT GOES FOR VICTINI AS WELL.
GOTHITELLE... DON'T BE TOO ROUGH. GENTLY DROP VICTINI INTO UNCONSCIOUSNESS.
IT APPEARS THAT VICTINI HAS FINALLY RUN OUT OF ENERGY AFTER THREE DAYS OF RUNNING FROM US.
FASSH
FLOP...

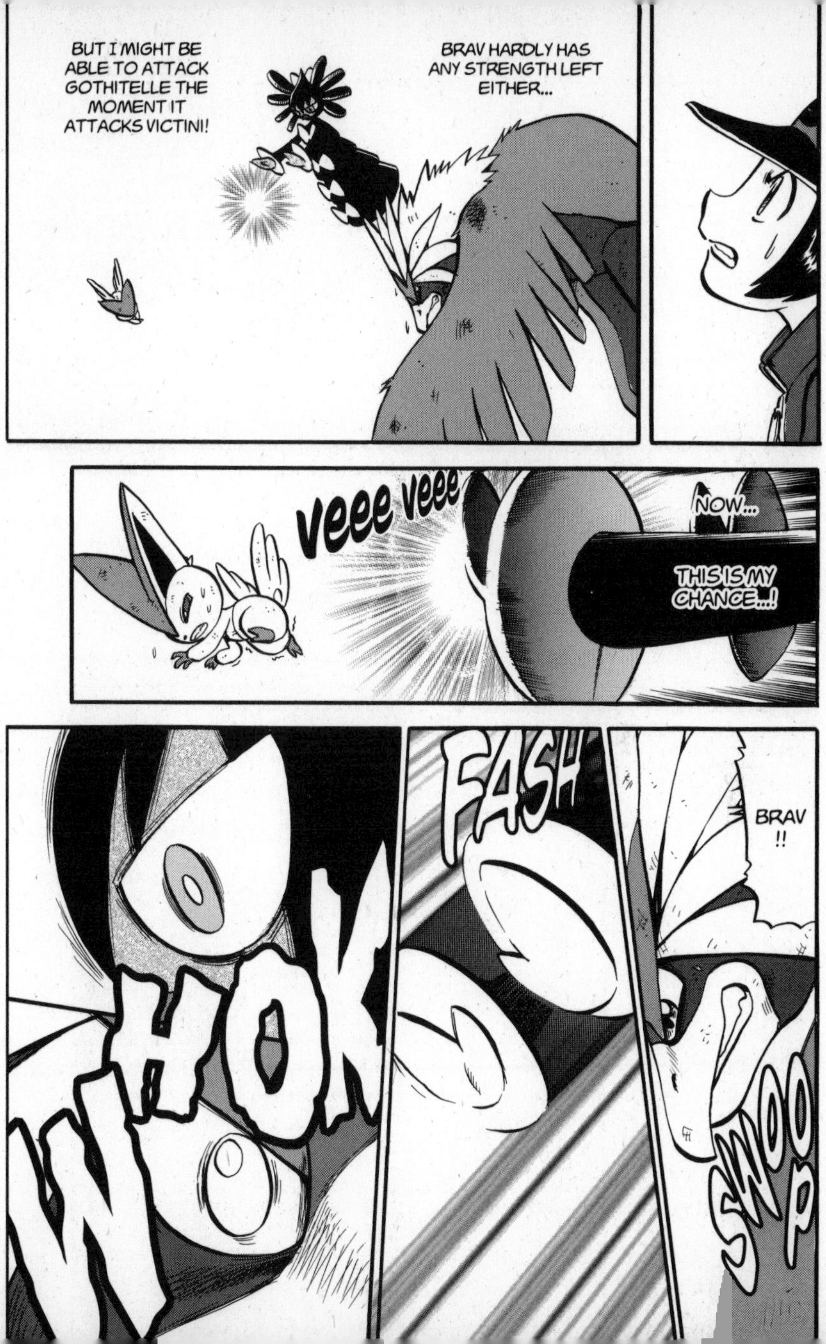
BRAV HARDLY HAS ANY STRENGTH LEFT EITHER...
BUT I MIGHT BE ABLE TO ATTACK GOTHITELLE THE MOMENT IT ATTACKS VICTINI!
NOW...
THIS IS MY CHANCE...!
veee veee
BRAV !!
FASH
WHOK
SWOOP

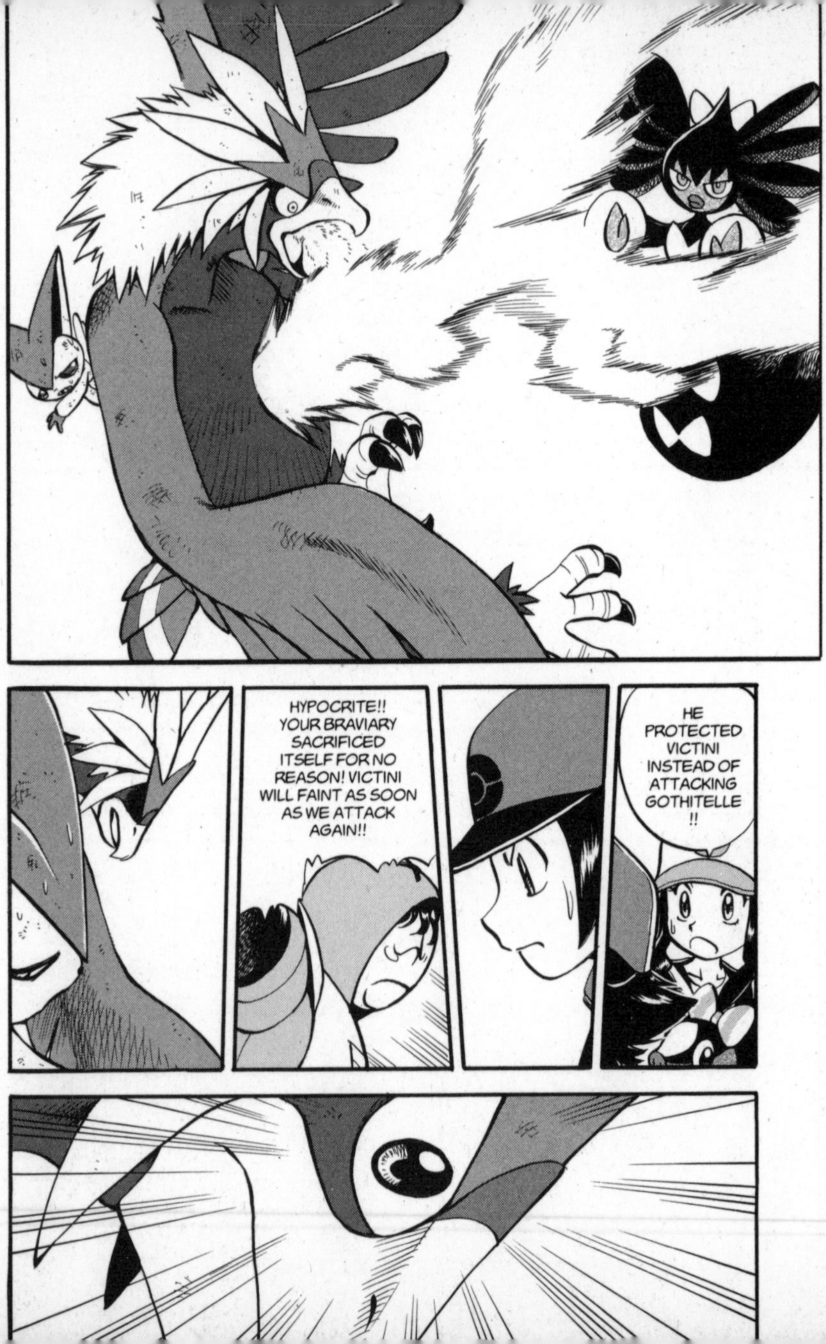
HE PROTECTED VICTINI INSTEAD OF ATTACKING GOTHITELLE !!
HYPOCRITE!! YOUR BRAVIARY SACRIFICED ITSELF FOR NO REASON! VICTINI WILL FAINT AS SOON AS WE ATTACK AGAIN!!

FAAAP

...WORKED!!

THE AT-TACK...

HUH ?!

H...

CHAK!

THOSE...

...WHO TOUCH IT...

IT CREATES AN UNLIMITED SUPPLY OF ENERGY INSIDE ITS BODY, WHICH IT SHARES WITH THOSE WHO TOUCH IT.

THIS POKÉMON BRINGS VICTORY.

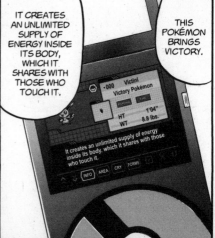

·000   Victini
       Victory Pokémon

HT   1'04"
WT   8.8 lbs.

It creates an unlimited supply of energy inside its body, which it shares with those who touch it.

INFO AREA CRY FORMS

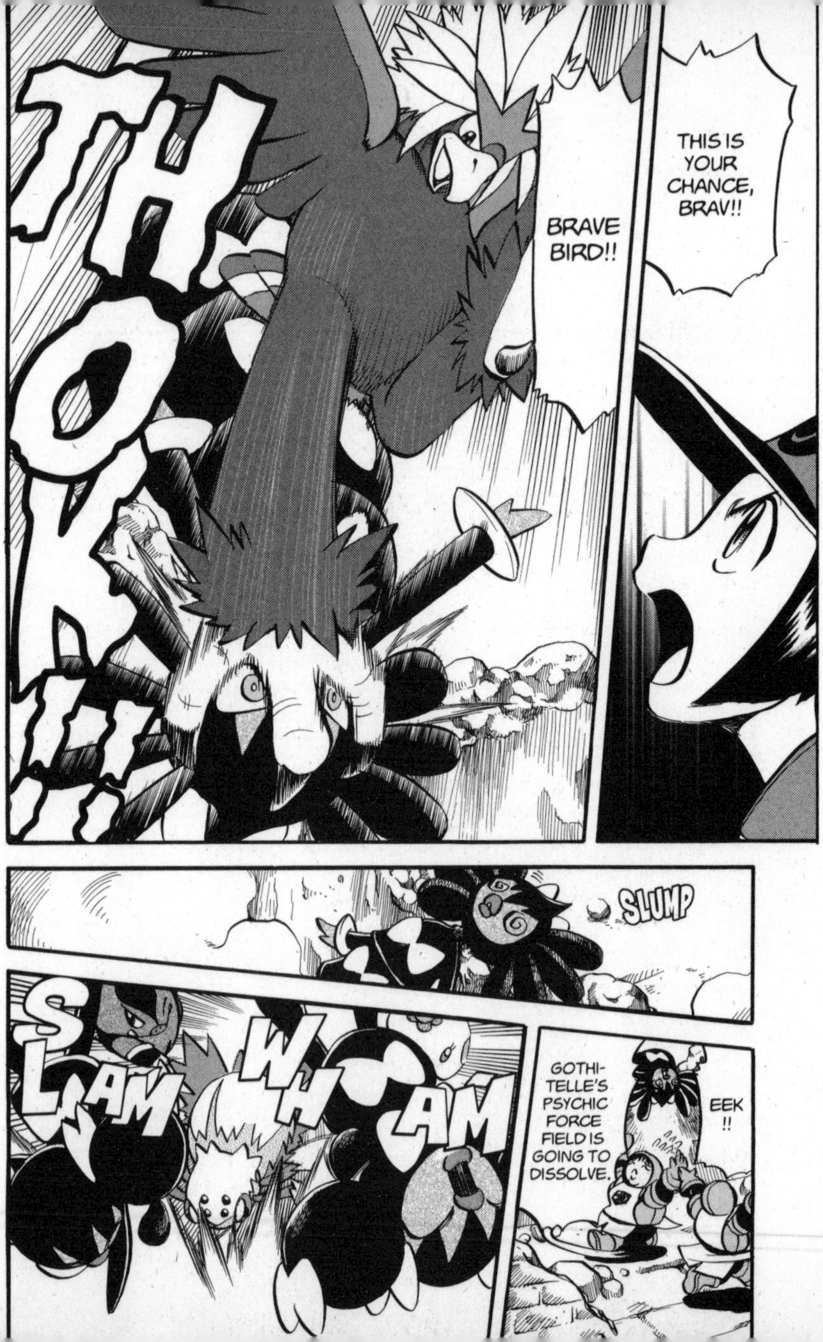

THIS IS YOUR CHANCE, BRAV!!
BRAVE BIRD!!
THOOM
SLUMP
EEK !!
GOTHI-TELLE'S PSYCHIC FORCE FIELD IS GOING TO DISSOLVE.
WHAM
SLAM

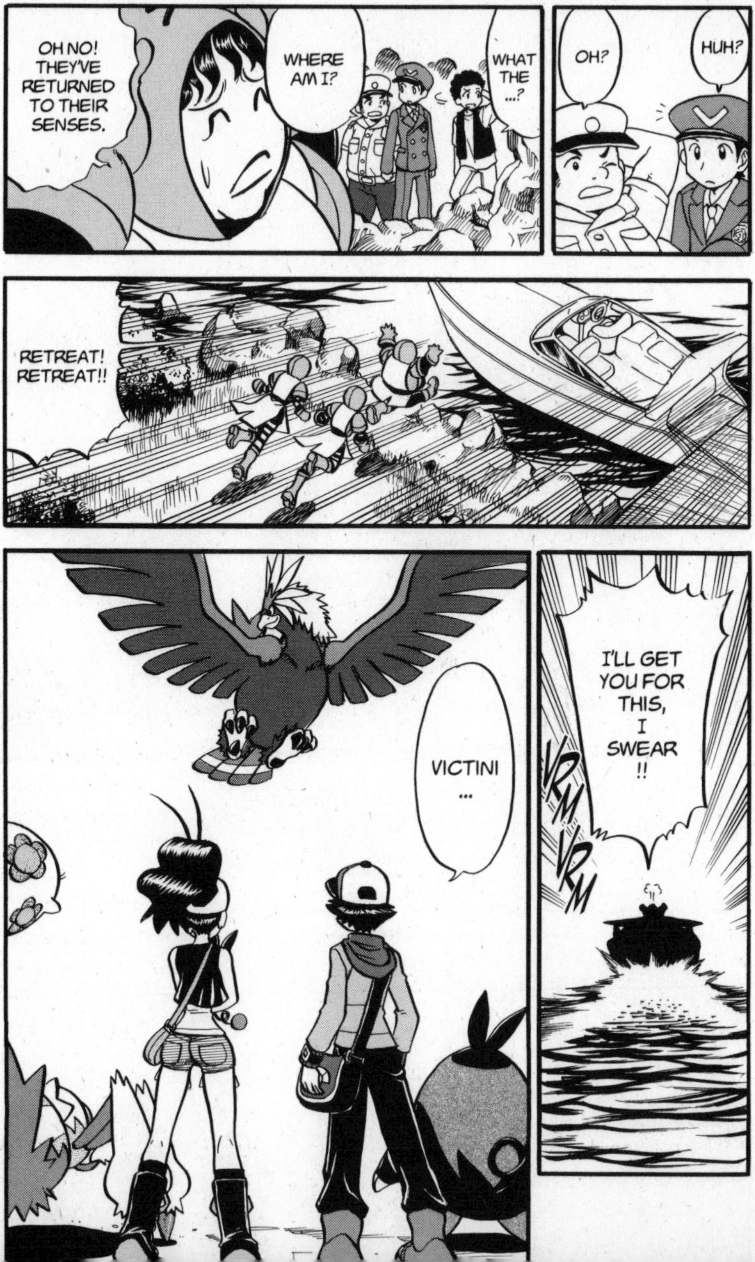
OH NO! THEY'VE RETURNED TO THEIR SENSES.
WHERE AM I?
WHAT THE ...?
OH?
HUH?
RETREAT! RETREAT!!
VICTINI ...
I'LL GET YOU FOR THIS, I SWEAR !!
VRM VRM VRM

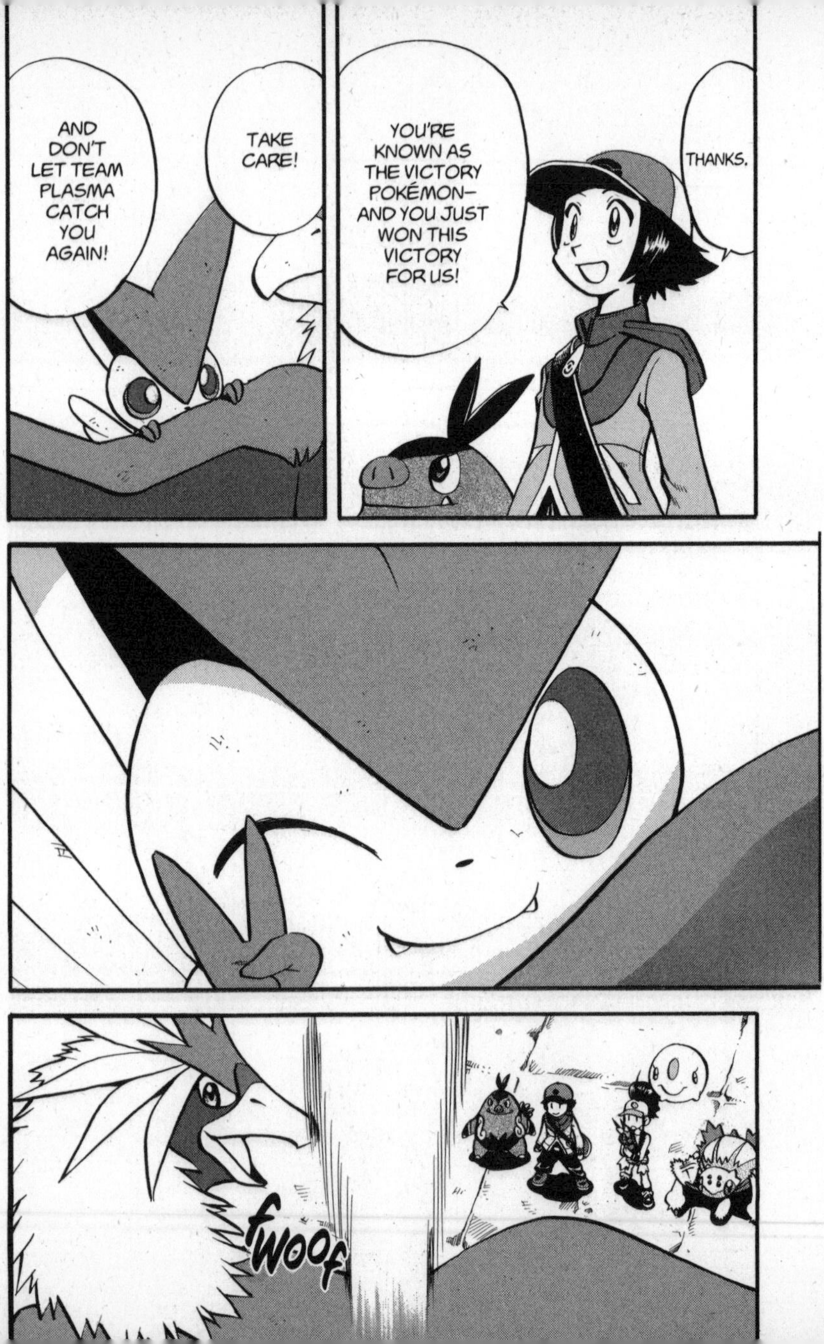
THANKS.
YOU'RE KNOWN AS THE VICTORY POKÉMON— AND YOU JUST WON THIS VICTORY FOR US!
TAKE CARE!
AND DON'T LET TEAM PLASMA CATCH YOU AGAIN!
FWOOF

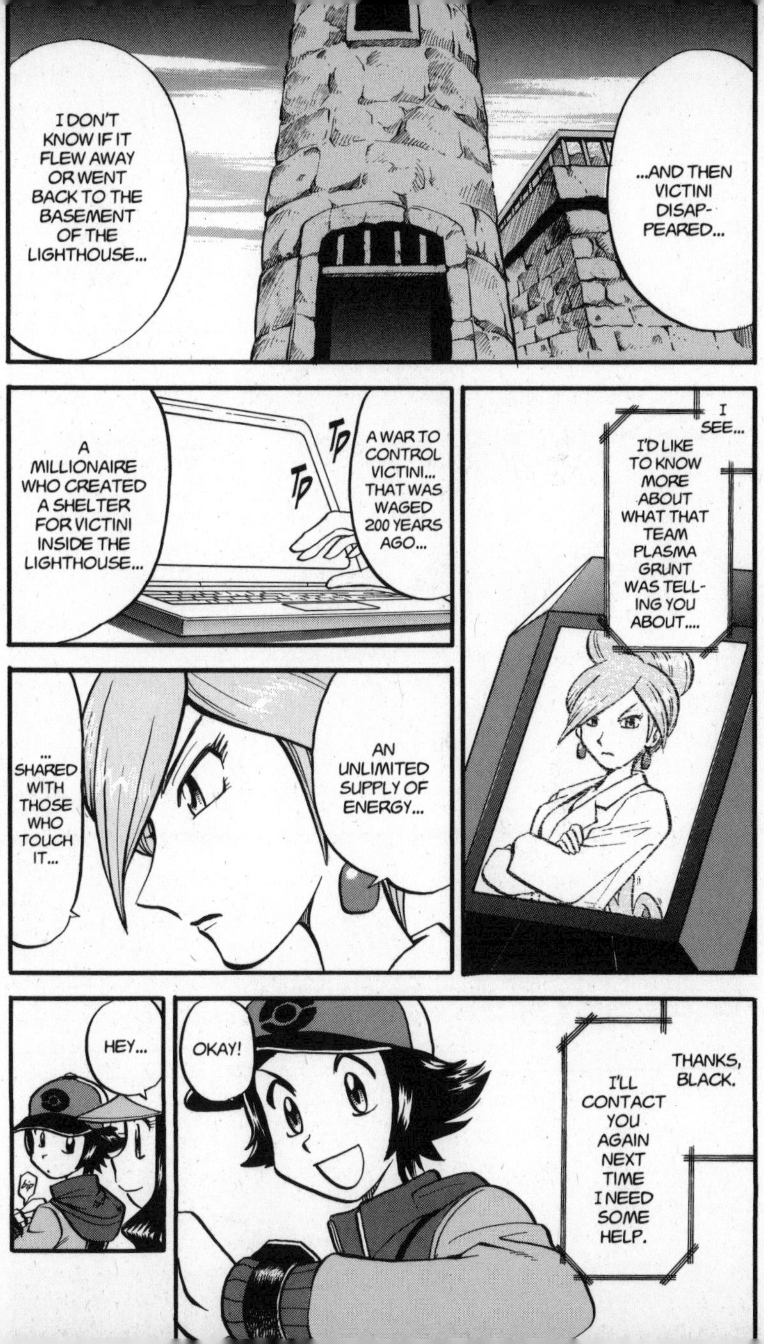

...AND THEN VICTINI DISAP-PEARED...
I DON'T KNOW IF IT FLEW AWAY OR WENT BACK TO THE BASEMENT OF THE LIGHTHOUSE...
I SEE...
I'D LIKE TO KNOW MORE ABOUT WHAT THAT TEAM PLASMA GRUNT WAS TELL-ING YOU ABOUT....
A WAR TO CONTROL VICTINI... THAT WAS WAGED 200 YEARS AGO...
TP
TP
A MILLIONAIRE WHO CREATED A SHELTER FOR VICTINI INSIDE THE LIGHTHOUSE...
AN UNLIMITED SUPPLY OF ENERGY...
...SHARED WITH THOSE WHO TOUCH IT...
THANKS, BLACK.
I'LL CONTACT YOU AGAIN NEXT TIME I NEED SOME HELP.
OKAY!
HEY...
bip

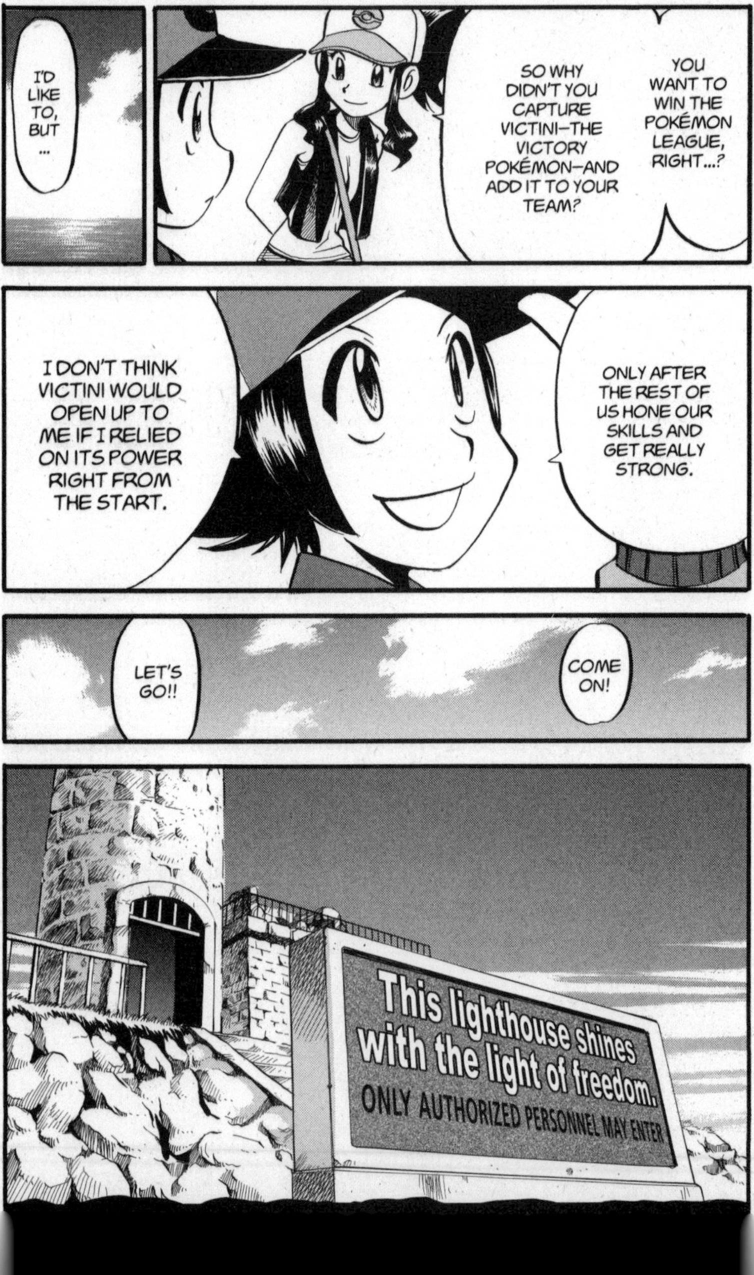

YOU WANT TO WIN THE POKÉMON LEAGUE, RIGHT...?
SO WHY DIDN'T YOU CAPTURE VICTINI—THE VICTORY POKÉMON—AND ADD IT TO YOUR TEAM?
I'D LIKE TO, BUT ...
I DON'T THINK VICTINI WOULD OPEN UP TO ME IF I RELIED ON ITS POWER RIGHT FROM THE START.
ONLY AFTER THE REST OF US HONE OUR SKILLS AND GET REALLY STRONG.
COME ON!
LET'S GO!!
This lighthouse shines with the light of freedom.
ONLY AUTHORIZED PERSONNEL MAY ENTER

More Adventures COMING SOON...

Black meets one of the Pokémon League Elite Four and strains his brain! The opening ceremony for White's Pokémon Musical is about to begin, but a critical element of the event is *missing*!

VOL. 7 AVAILABLE MAY 2012!

The Struggle for Time and Space Begins Again!

Available at a DVD retailer near you!

Pokémon Trainer Ash and his Pikachu must find the Jewel of Life and stop Arceus from devastating all existence! The journey will be both dangerous and uncertain: even if Ash and his friends can set an old wrong right again, will there be time to return the Jewel of Life before Arceus destroys everything and everyone they've ever known?

Manga edition also available from VIZ Media

POKÉMON
ARCEUS
AND THE
JEWEL OF LIFE

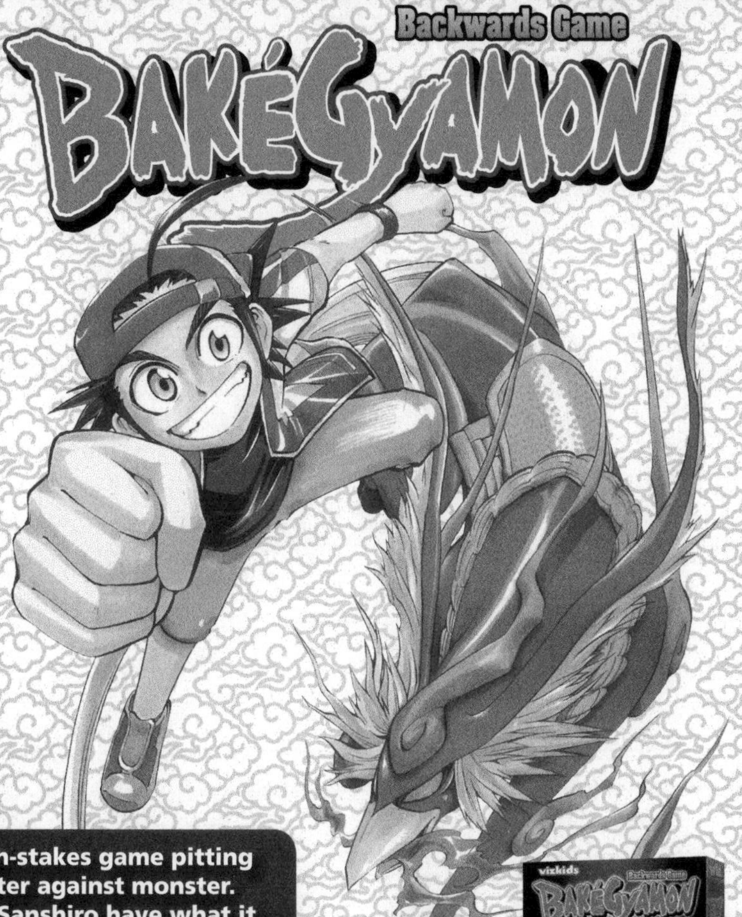
Backwards Game
BAKÉGYAMON
vizkids
Backwards Game
BAKÉGYAMON
1

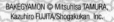

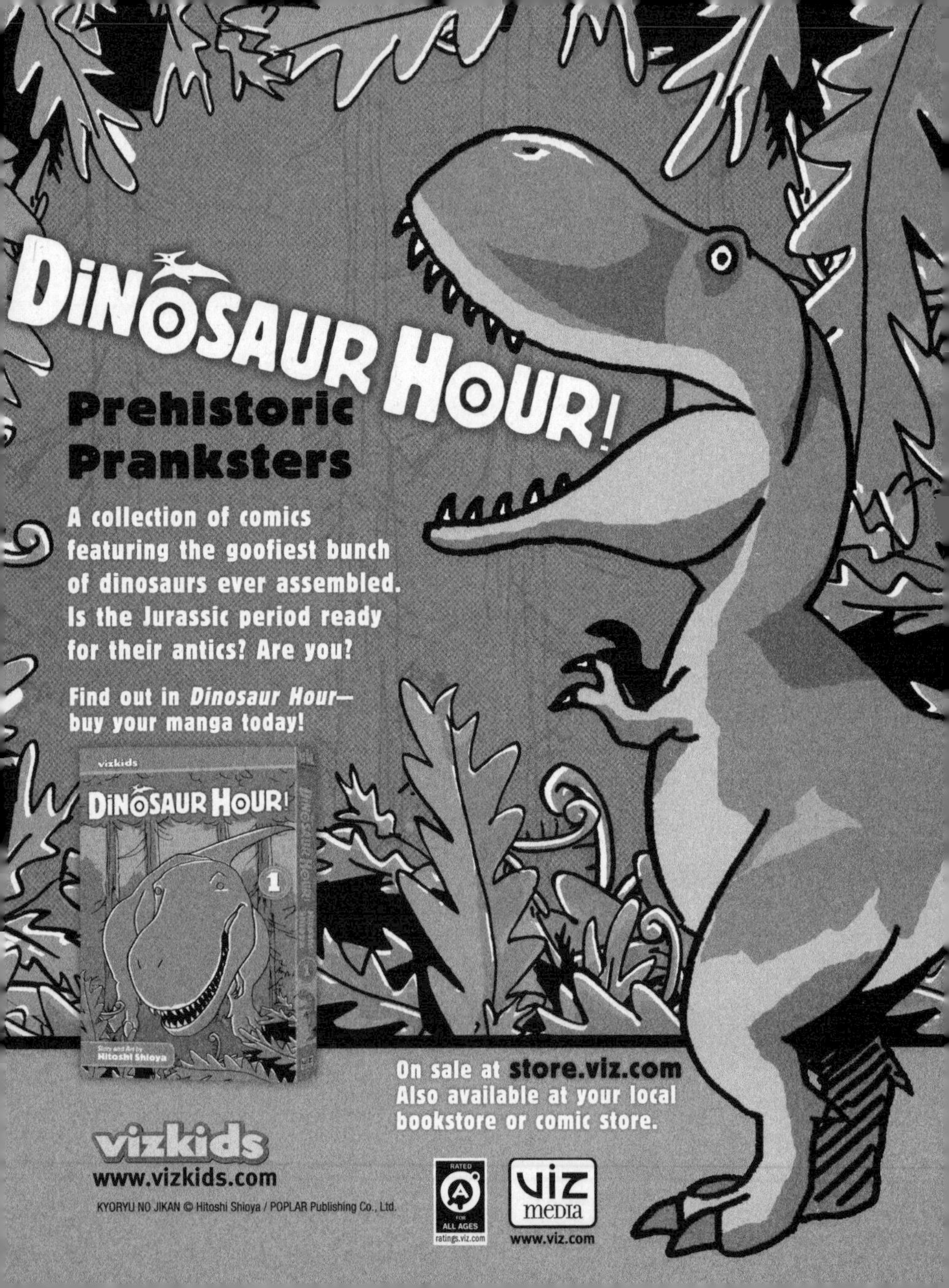
DINOSAUR HOUR!
Prehistoric Pranksters
A collection of comics featuring the goofiest bunch of dinosaurs ever assembled. Is the Jurassic period ready for their antics? Are you?
Find out in *Dinosaur Hour*—buy your manga today!
vizkids
DINOSAUR HOUR!
1
Hitoshi Shioya
On sale at store.viz.com
Also available at your local bookstore or comic store.
vizkids
www.vizkids.com
KYORYU NO JIKAN © Hitoshi Shioya / POPLAR Publishing Co., Ltd.
RATED
A
FOR ALL AGES
ratings.viz.com
VIZ media
www.viz.com

What's Better Than Catching Pokémon? Becoming one!

Pokémon Mystery Dungeon
GINJI'S RESCUE TEAM

Ginji is a normal boy until the day he turns into a Torchic and joins Mudkip's Rescue Team. Now he must help any and all Pokémon in need...but will Ginji be able to rescue his human self?

Become part of the adventure—and mystery—with *Pokémon Mystery Dungeon: Ginji's Rescue Team.* Buy yours today!

www.pokemon.com

Take a trip with Pokémon
ALL THAT PIKACHU!
ANI-MANGA™

Meet Pikachu and all-star Pokémon! Two complete Pikachu stories taken from the Pokémon movies—all in a full color manga.

Buy yours today!

Pokémon
www.pokemon.com

vizkids

VIZ
media
www.viz.com